TRANSFORMATION

DREYA LOVE BOOK 1

DANA LYONS

Copyright © 2018 by Dana Lyons

All rights reserved.

This is a work of fiction. Names, places, characters and incidents are the product of the author's imagination or are used fictitiously. Any resemblance to any actual persons, living or dead is entirely coincidental.

All rights reserved under the International and Pan-American Copyright Conventions. No part of this book may be reproduced or transmitted in any form or by any means, electronic or mechanical, including photocopying, recording, or by any information storage and retrieval system, without permission in writing from the publisher.

No part of this book may be reproduced including information storage and retrieval systems, without written permission from the author, except for the use of brief quotations in a book review.

Cover design by Ivan Zanchetta

1

DRACO STATION OVER THE PLANET DRACO PRIME

"ALL THOSE YEARS IN SCHOOL FOR A CHEMISTRY DEGREE AND now I'm a thief," Gideon mumbled. He glanced up and down the hallway of the genetics lab, making sure no one else was about. "It's 3:00 A.M., everyone should be in bed."

He slid his access-card through the lock and the door silently opened. Staying in the dark, he made another quick glance about and moved to the door of Dr. Lazar's office. He reached quietly into his pocket for a fake ID card and slid it. When the office door opened, he stepped inside and pressed himself against the wall. His heart pounded wildly and sweat ran down his face. He wiped himself on his shirt sleeve, clearing his eyes. "One, two, three," he counted. "Relax. No one's here, just get the formula and disappear tomorrow going back to Earth."

With no light, he stepped to Lazar's desk, his hands seeking a path across the furniture in the dark. He found the chair and sat, wiping his face again. He pulled a small light from a pocket and shined it onto the locked safe to the right of the chair. He entered the code for the safe as he whispered, "Nice and easy. I get caught and I'm stuck in this rat hole for life."

The safe opened and he reached into the top shelf as he shined the light over the contents. "There, right where I expected it to be."

As he grabbed the Nobility sample, the overhead light came on. He looked up, heart slamming against his breast bone, certain Lazar had caught him. "Oh, hey Annie. What are you doing here at this hour?" He edged his hand towards his pants and slipped the Nobility drug sample into his pocket. He turned off the little light and put it into the other pant pocket as he closed the safe door and stood.

Annie was a cleaner. She should have been finished and gone hours ago. He moved with authority towards the door and motioned her to step back into the lab, closing Lazar's office door. She might not be Lazar, but she was just as bad.

"I forgot to dust Lazar's office. I was just getting ready to turn out my lights when I remembered. You know what a stinker he can be when something isn't done." She waved a bucket of cleaning supplies in one hand and her ring of master keys in the other hand. She stood by the office door, one hip cocked and a nasty grin on her face. "What are you doing here in the Doc's office at—" She glanced at her watch. " 3:30?"

She craned her neck and peeked at his pocket, now bulging with the Nobility sample he just stole. His brain ran fast, looking for an answer. He walked away from the door, moving into the genetics work space. "I had some notes to clear up before I leave tomorrow. Back to Earth, you know."

She was grandfathered in from Hammer Industries, her family 2 generations into the station. She'd never go back to

Earth. But if she snitched on him, he would never go back to Earth either. A shiver ran up his back. Being caught thieving Nobility would see him genetically modified into a dragon and kept in poverty quarters on the lowest level for decades until he finally died. A harsh taste flooded his mouth—the last thing he wanted was to be shackled down in purgatory for the rest of his life.

"Clearing up notes, huh?" she said, a sneer replacing the grin on her face. "Is that the notes you have?" She dropped her bucket and reached towards his pants pocket.

They stood in a passageway that angled upwards, the flooring a rubber mat. The horror of life on Draco was a pressure in his mind. He remembered always tripping on the rubber mat and nearly bashing his head on the wall when he first arrived. He shifted sideways from her and suddenly shoved her into the steel wall. She bounced off with a squeal, grabbing her bleeding head. He rammed her head into the wall again with all his might and she slumped to the floor.

He quickly turned off the overhead light and shrank down out of sight by anyone who might be walking by. He checked Annie's pulse, but she was dead. "No, no, no," he mumbled, but it was too late.

Annie was dead.

He was a thief and a murderer.

Earth was a long way off.

Washington, D.C.

. . .

On the last day of her life, young Libby Stanton was a woman on a mission. She turned in front of the mirror in her Georgetown apartment, admiring her reflection, smoothing her dress down over her hips. A diamond pendant glittered at her throat, with matching studs in her ears. Her purse, shoes and dress were all assembled to create maximum effect—exposure and attention.

"This ought to get a rise," she predicted. She made a pout and fluffed her hair, remembering the words she heard in the bathroom at Smith Point last night.

"He's coming back on the market," a young female voice said.

"Yeah, I heard he's done with Libby and her ways."

Giggle giggle snicker snicker.

Libby's pout faltered. She shivered as the chill of rejection slipped over her shoulders. Her lover had been acting ... difficult lately.

"Well," she brightened and announced to her reflection. "I can't have him breaking up with me."

She dialed his number and tapped her foot with agitation until he answered. "Oh, hi, honey. I'm ready. Yes, the George tonight. It should be packed. Okay. See you in a few."

She checked her reflection a last time and approved.

No one dumps the senator's daughter.

He arrived at her door, the perfect gentleman ... with a secret behind his brown eyes. Still, she smiled and greeted him warmly, needing this to go strictly as planned. "Hey baby, you look nice tonight."

"And you, too," he answered.

He raked her up and down, perhaps, she wondered, regretting his decision to break up with her. Too bad. Once news hits the gossip mongers, it passes the point of no return.

Their brief ride to the club reeked of words unspoken, past, present and future. Libby glanced at him, speculating who he planned to meet after breaking up with her. Well, she thought, *he'll never get the chance*. Keeping to her plan, she judiciously maintained tight lips.

At the club, her face was so well known she didn't have to flash her little member card. They cruised by the long line and she nodded to the bouncer; he unclipped the velvet rope.

She walked ahead, scanning the crowd, looking for anyone she knew with a cell phone ready to take a photo or video. In the corner was a table of fashion models; she waved even though she hated them. But she knew that long-legged little brunette was jealous of her status and would no doubt be quick to capture any action. Libby could see the headline in the Daily Gossip tomorrow, *Libby Stanton Throws Drink in Lover's Face, Storms Out.*

"Perrier, no lime," she ordered.

Her drink came and with it a lull in the music as the DJ lined up a new set. The moment was perfect. She stood and picked up her drink.

He's lucky I didn't order a Singapore Sling.

She tossed the glass of iced Perrier in his face, taking a long second to appreciate his stunned expression ... and for the flashes to announce the event was well recorded. "No one dumps the senator's daughter," she declared loud enough for all to hear. She collected her bag and sauntered out, giving him a long view of what he would never know again.

Leaving him with her head held high and a smile on her face was exhilarating. Such a public display made her heart pound with excitement; she knew her actions would make tomorrow's news.

Outside the club, she drew a deep breath, fanning her face until her nerves settled. At last her heart slowed and the adrenaline rush faded. A glance at her watch showed a little past midnight. "Hmm, where shall I go?" She pulled out her cell phone when a male voice asked, "Do you need a ride?"

She looked up. Shiny new car pulled to the curb; passenger window down; driver in his thirties, well dressed and cute with deep eyes. "Oh? And who are you?" She kept one eye on him while she scanned her contacts list.

He smiled, revealing a charming dimple. "I'm a man who sees a beautiful lady dressed for a party. In need of company? I was just about to go in."

Going back in was the last thing on her mind. But his voice was smooth and his tone disarming. She slipped her phone back into her bag. "It's an ugly crowd in there tonight. That's why I left."

He popped the door lock. "Then we'll go somewhere else."

She gave him another inspection; he really was cute. "Tell me, handsome, what do you do?"

"I'm a man of science. Come have a drink with me Miss ...?"

A ripple of delight ran up her spine and she smiled broadly. When she was a child, she always liked listening to the science people when they came to talk to her father. Men who spoke with big words made her feel safe and protected. "I'm Libby." She reached for the door.

"Welcome Libby. My name's Gideon. Gideon Smith."

Transformation 7

Libby strolled through the door into Gideon's fashionable home. This sudden turn of events was pleasing, with the night evolving into a wining situation. He was cute, educated, well mannered, and seemed financially secure. While she originally planned to have a drink with him and then call for a ride, she was beginning to see the advantages of staying longer.

He stopped at a bar station in the corner of the kitchen. "What would you like to drink?"

"Can you make me a margarita? On the rocks, with salt? And I'd like to use the bathroom."

"Sure, I can make the margarita," he said eagerly. "That's my drink. You'll find a bathroom," he pointed, "down that hall on the left."

As she wandered through the house she was intrigued, seeing a tasteful living room filled with furniture and respectable art. She bypassed the bathroom and ventured further down the hall to the main bedroom. "Hmm, maybe I will stay," she murmured, eyeing the cozy king bed. She stepped into the spacious bath. A nice Jacuzzi tub. "Perhaps, after a couple margaritas."

She placed her purse on the counter and stepped back from the mirror to take a selfie. "There," she confirmed. Judging the photo worthwhile, she saved it. In the photo's background, she noticed an oddity.

"What's that?" On a shelf behind her was a curio, something like a snow globe only red, not white. She picked it up, shook it, and watched the red flakes dance around a volcano. "Isn't that bizarre." She returned the globe to its place on the shelf.

Going back to the mirror, she cleaned the corners of her eyes and examined her face again. A little lipstick, a touch of bronzer followed by a swipe through her hair with her fingertips, and she beamed with satisfaction. "I am margarita ready."

She reached to pick up her cell phone when her hand began shaking. The tremor visibly traveled up her arm and spread across her body. "What?" she mumbled, grabbing the counter top and knocking her phone across the hard surface to fly off the edge. Her tremors rapidly increased. She wanted to cry out, but her throat was blocked.

Can't breathe!

She slid to the tile floor and tried to claw at her throat, but full-body convulsions held her muscles rigid. "Gecyk," she croaked. Sparkles filled her vision. She desperately wanted to stand and run, to go home and change into her robe. But the only sound she could make was, "Gecyk."

Heat coursed through her body. She was on fire inside. Blistering, raging and molten, her blood bubbled, making her want to shriek. Excruciating pain rushed through her bones. Her skin was a blistering bed of prickly cactus. The sparkles in her eyes overtook her vision and merged into a field of white. She kicked spasmodically several times. Her eyes rolled back. Her bladder released.

In the kitchen, Gideon cheerfully mixed the margaritas. He hummed as he carried the drinks in search of miss hottie, "Libby." He couldn't believe his luck crossing her path; the prospects of getting laid were looking good.

The living room was empty so he cruised down the hall to the bathroom. Also, empty. "Hmmm, dare I hope?" He walked on to his bedroom. In the doorway he called, "Libby?"

No one in the bed. "Maybe she's in the hot tub already." He went towards the bathroom. When he saw her on the floor, he shrieked. She was clearly dead, the whites of her eyes showing, her body contorted. "Damn, what the hell?"

He set the drinks down and stepped back, staring at her. "What? Was she high on something before we got here?"

He gingerly stepped over her body, trying not to look at the foam on her red lips, the blood at her nose, the puddle that leaked out from beneath her dress. From one of the drawers, he extracted a long cotton swab and nudged around in her purse.

No drugs in there.

"What, what, what do I do?" he moaned.

Libby's dead body stirred memories of his last night on Draco Station. Only the dead body that night was Annie Cooper. "She caught me stealing. I had no choice but to kill her," he blurted, struggling for redemption. Remorse for the past and fear for the future suddenly ripped through him. "Annie, I got away with your murder—but this ..."

Abruptly he bent over, his stomach threatening to hurl its bare contents. Water flooded his eyes and he swallowed bile. The miserable irony of the situation was not lost on him.

The accidental death leads directly to the murder.

Worrying the problem in his head, he paced. "What the hell killed you, Libby? Why were you back here?" He glanced around; his eyes fell on the snow globe from Draco Station. "Oh shit, did she touch that?"

He slapped his forehead several times. "Think, think. Did I screw up the transfer when I removed the drug from the globe?" He remembered the day he extracted the small sample of Lazar's Nobility drug. The bag seemed intact, but maybe there was a tiny hole and his gloves got contaminated.

"Dammit, dammit, dammit," he cursed through stiff lips. He walked to the bedroom and stared at her body, his hand pressed to his forehead. "I have a dead body." He moaned, "This is not my fault," and started pacing.

Seeing his life fly by as a pretty boy in prison, he added, "I am so screwed over this." He scrubbed at his face, searching for a way out. "Okay, she's on a tile floor and there's no massive blood spill. We haven't even kissed, so there's minimal DNA transfer."

The pacing began again. Gradually a plan formed. He stopped and patted down his pockets for keys. "Don't go anywhere, Libby. I'll be right back."

Two hours later he returned, raising the garage door with the remote and driving in. "Whoa," he gasped. He let his head drop back against the headrest, sucking air as if he'd held his breath the entire time he was gone. Mutely, he offered his excuse for a prayer, knowing he was in a dubious position to be seeking heavenly assistance.

Still. Everyone needs help at some point.

He carried in his purchases. Putting on gloves, he unwrapped and rolled out a tarp next to Libby's body, and placed a newly purchased rug on top of the tarp.

"There you go, Libby." He dragged her body onto the rug and rolled her up. Using the tarp as a sled, he hauled the rug down the hall, across the kitchen and through the garage. He stuffed the assemblage into the trunk of his car, slammed the trunk lid, and sat on it, panting from his exertions. When he caught his breath, he lamented angrily, "Damn. Looks like I'm not getting laid tonight. Now what?"

Tapping a worried finger on the trunk, he recalled a dark stretch along the river in Anacostia Park. "Yep. As good a place as any to dump her."

2

FBI Special Agent Dreya Love woke slowly. With her eyes still closed, she assessed her situation. She was in a bed, but the sheets smelled of a different laundry detergent than she used.

Not home.

A mental check of her body revealed rather well-used parts down below. She scrunched her face in an effort to recall who ... when a vision came to mind clearly substantiating her suspicions, one of bodies straining in the throes of a very athletic sexual act.

She opened one eye. Seeing nothing scary, she opened the other eye. She didn't recognize anything as the lights were off when she and ... someone tumbled in here. A man's shoe and a pair of briefs on the floor gave her a clue.

Proof of life came from another room. Sounds, movement, water running. The smell of coffee and ... bacon? "Is he cooking?" she mumbled. "Dear God, let me get out of here." She rolled over to search for her clothing and a clock. "Five-thirty. Who the hell eats at five-thirty in the morning?"

In the corner, she spotted a pile of clothes with a red

high-heel shoe. "Ah." Finally, something familiar. She crawled out of bed and slinked hunched over to pick up her clothes. Her dress slipped on over her head. With one heel in her hand, she went to her knees searching under the bed for her panties. "Found you," she said, clutching them in her hand.

Pushing her hair out of her eyes, she sat back on her haunches. A rather impressive male form suddenly filled her vision. "Oh. It's you. Hi." She couldn't remember his name. While he was tall, dark and gorgeous, she guessed he had Sunday morning plans. Food, more sex, talk …

Sorry to disappoint.

She was not good at post-coital hugging, nor did she draw pleasure from the inane pleasantries of sharing food and revealing one's deepest secrets. She shivered at the thought.

"Dreya, your phone's been vibrating since five o'clock." He passed it to her. As if responding to his words, it hummed like an angry bee. She took the phone, wondering if he deliberately stated her name because he knew she didn't recall his.

Her phone screen indicated a dozen predawn calls on a Sunday morning; her heart hammered with anxiety. "This is not good." The phone jumped in her hands and she accepted the incoming call from her boss, Assistant Director in Charge of the DC office. "This is Love."

"Dreya, where are you?"

His use of her first name was an alarm in itself. She inhaled sharply. "Not home, sir. What's happening?" She closed her eyes with the familiar prayer.

Please, no, let it not be …

"I need you at a crime scene." His tone shifted and his

next words made her cringe that he knew her so well. "Do you have to go home first?"

She looked down at the panties and shoe in her hand. "Yes, sir. What's happened?"

Tall, dark, and gorgeous leaned against the door jamb frowning, no doubt sensing his Sunday morning plans gone awry. While she was thankful to be relieved from this engaging play, she hated that her escape was delivered at the cost of someone's life.

"Go home," Jarvis ordered. "Change clothes. Call me then."

"Sir," she blurted, but he had hung up.

"Bad news?" gorgeous asked.

"Yes." She avoided his eye; she just wanted to go. "I'll call you," she said as she grabbed her other shoe and stopped long enough to step into her panties. She darted past him, picked her purse from the kitchen counter, and made for the door.

"I haven't given you my number," he called out.

"It's okay," she said over her shoulder as she stepped out the door. "I'm the FBI."

DC METRO DETECTIVE RHYS MORGAN LEANED AGAINST THE fender of his car looking down at the sticky mud accumulating on his fine leather shoes. A hum of activity filled the riverside area, with several police cars, a paramedic van and a coroner's vehicle all flashing their lights. At this ungodly hour, a mist rose from the river, putting a chill in the air.

"What a mess," he groused under his breath. His phone rang. "Morgan," he answered. Hearing his boss's voice only deepened the unhappy scowl digging deep into his face. "No Chief, the Feds aren't here yet. Yes, I'm keeping the scene tight. Of course, I'll let you know when they get here." He looked up and saw a pair of standard federal agency vehicles pull in. "Oh, goody, Chief," he reported. "The cavalry has arrived."

A black man got out of the first car and waited for the driver of the second car. Rhys leaned over to see, expecting a standard issue, slick suited Fed prototype to emerge. What came instead was—

His mouth dropped open. The Fed was a woman, and she was not a standard issue anything. She had long honey blonde hair, green eyes, and a strut that belonged in high-heels. He clamped his lips tight and closed his eyes, wanting to scrub her image from his mind. "No freaking way."

Dreya pulled into the crime scene with its maze of multi-agency uniforms, flashing lights, and yards of yellow crime scene tape. Swallowing her trepidation, she met with her boss, Herb Jarvis. "Director, what's all the secrecy? High profile?"

She nodded toward the tarp covered area shielding the victim's body. Jarvis' earlier obfuscation on the phone about this victim had her on edge. She wanted to jerk the tarp back and face whatever her boss was trying to prepare her for.

Just tell me. Get it over with.

When he spoke, she regretted the thought.

"Dreya, it's Libby."

As soon as the words came out of his mouth, she stepped back. "No." She shook her head in denial. "No, not Libby." She turned and walked towards her car, putting her back to the crime scene. Tears sprouted in her eyes, and she looked up to keep them from falling. But fall they did, coursing down her face until she flipped them off her chin.

Get it together.

She wiped her face on her sleeve and straightened herself mentally. For a moment she stood, one hand on her hip, collecting her thoughts, controlling the rage she felt every time she came to the murder scene of an innocent. That this innocent was a young woman she knew should not affect her performance. She exhaled deeply and pushed her guilt and grief into another dimension.

I'm sorry I wasn't there for you this time, Libby.

Jarvis waited for her.

She returned to his side. "What can you tell me?" She braced herself.

"There is no external trauma. First we'll rule out suicide."

No chance of that, she thought. Libby was too full of life. She sighed, deeply grateful she didn't have Libby's bludgeoned, stabbed or eviscerated corpse to deal with. A quick glance at the strong show of uniforms prompted her to ask, "Who's the lead on this?"

"Rhys Morgan, Metro PD. That's him leaning on the car."

She squinted and tilted her head, checking out Detective Morgan. Her first thought was *what a handsome man*—black hair, sculpted face, tall and lean. But the stink-eye he threw at her caused her to change her assessment. "He doesn't look too happy to see us."

"Are they ever?" Jarvis said.

They walked over and Jarvis made the introduction. When he said her name, Morgan's unhappy face grew even darker. A handshake was not offered.

Dreya snorted.

Whatever, man. Maybe he's just not a morning person.

She stared at Libby's covered body. Morgan removed his notepad, reading. "Caucasian female, mid-twenties, she is the daughter of—"

His deadpan tone irritated her. While she didn't expect him to feel her grief over this lost life, still his demeanor was irksome. She cut him off. "She's the daughter of Senator Stanton. I know the victim, Detective Morgan."

She walked off, leaving him with Jarvis as she approached the tarp. Murder and mayhem were old friends of hers; she had seen more bodies than she wanted to count. But rarely, thank goodness, did she find someone she cared about under the tarp.

Except for today.

She put on gloves, squatted down and pulled the tarp back. At the sight of Libby's face, she gasped and closed her eyes.

She did not have an easy death.

While Libby's body was saved from the effects of a long-term immersion, her face was locked in a rigor of pain and terror. "Dear Libby, what did you do?" She pulled the cover all the way back to reveal the body, looking not only at what was there, but evaluating what was missing. After walking around slowly, she stopped, propping up one arm while her finger tapped on her chin.

There were no clamoring surprises on Libby's body. The dress, the make-up, her one shoe. She made a mental notation about the missing shoe. On the other side of the body, she squatted down to get a closer look. Seeing something shiny, she reached between Libby's breasts where the dress plunged low.

"What the hell?" What caught her eye appeared to be a

feather, a tiny, baby feather. She intended to lift it away from the body, but it was attached.

"Huh," she grunted. A quick look about showed no one interested in what she was doing. Detective Scowl-face had his back to her and was speaking animatedly to one of the medical examiner's team. Jarvis was glued to his phone, staring heavenward, a finger pressed into his free ear.

She pulled lightly on the feather, it was definitely attached. A quick tug and it came free with a tiny 'pop'. She dug out an evidence bag, dropped the feather in it and slipped the bag back in her pocket.

"What else is wrong here?" she mumbled. She peered at the flesh of Libby's arm and squinted, not sure what she was seeing. The skin was ... shadowed.

She replaced the tarp, covering Libby's twisted face, her contorted body, her blank eyes. "Don't you worry, honey," she said as she stood. "Someone sure as hell is going to pay for this."

Jarvis was motioning her to join him. As she arrived, he finished his phone conversation, nodding his head. "Yes, sir, Senator Stanton. I understand. I'll tell her." He put the phone in his pocket.

"What?"

"The senator wants you on this."

She shrugged. "I expected that; I wouldn't have it any other way."

"He wants you to work with Morgan. He knows the Detective from a prior case, and he wants him to be a part of the investigation."

Jarvis pulled her off to the side. "What the senator wants, he gets. He wants you because he knows you and he knows your ... level of integrity." He looked at her pointedly. "He also knows you're working without a partner."

She sighed, knowing a not-so-subtle reprimand was coming from Jarvis and stared over his shoulder at Detective Morgan. The detective spoke with the medical examiner. Jarvis' voice droned on.

"Everyone at the Bureau applauds you turning in your partner for corruption, but you can't keep working alone."

Focused on Morgan, she responded in robotic tones. "Not my fault no one wants to work with me."

He pulled her closer and hissed in her ear. "You went over the line when you gave that recording to your partner's wife and you damn well know it."

"What I damn well know," she hissed in return, "is his wife needed to understand what she was married to." She pulled back and looked him up and down, sticking her chin out in defiance. "I'd do it again."

He ignored her challenge. "Because of Libby's identity, this case is Federal, so you're in charge. But know this is your last case without a partner—you need to prepare yourself for that eventuality." He jerked his head toward Morgan. "Work with the detective because Stanton demands it. And work with him because you need to freshen up your people skills."

She puffed up with indignation, but kept her silence, letting Jarvis blather on. Behind him, Detective Morgan's antics were regaling the medical examiner.

"Are you listening to me?"

Bolting back to the moment, she saw Jarvis' mouth in a flat, grim line, a sure sign she had missed something. "Yes, sir. Of course, I am. You were saying?"

"I was saying this is your last case working alone; I can't have you going rogue any longer. After this, you take the next test and advance, or I'm parking you with a partner on the backside of hell. Understand?"

She blinked, wondering what fulfilled Jarvis' idea of the backside of hell. She didn't want to know. "Yes, sir."

"Keep me posted, and go work with your new partner." He stalked over to his car and drove off.

"Whew," she exhaled with a whistle. Eyeing Morgan and the ME, she approached, her lips clamped tight in expectation of Morgan's attitude. Whatever his problem was, he'd better get over it quick.

The ME saw her and nodded to Morgan, who turned and watched her walk up; the smile and animation drained from his face with her every step. By the time she reached him, his eyes were hard, his lips in a rigid line of disapproval, and his hands shoved in his pockets.

She ignored him. She pulled out her notepad and spoke to the medical examiner. "Time of death?"

"Time of death, factoring in the length of immersion and the water temperature—"

"Yeah, yeah," she said, turning her finger in a circle to speed him along.

"About 1:00 A.M., maybe a little earlier. Baring suicide—"

"Libby Stanton did not commit suicide." The ME shot her a quick glance. "I know her," she protested. "This is not a suicide."

"Then with no obvious fatal wounds, COD will likely turn up in the toxicology report. I'll know more when I get her open, but I'm betting the answers are in toxicology. It always tells the tale."

She thought of the tiny feather she plucked from Libby's breast.

Going to be one hell of a tale.

During this conversation, she kept Morgan in her peripheral vision. He stepped back and leaned against the vehicle, ankles crossed, hands still stuffed in his pockets, chin high ... looking down his nose at her in a most condescending way.

He's gonna' fool around and piss me off.

She focused on staying professional and directed her next questions at Morgan. "Are there any witnesses? Do we know when and where she entered the water? Was a purse found? Cell phone?"

He uncrossed his ankles and pushed off from the fender, bringing his chin down to answer her. "No. No and no. No. No."

She closed her eyes and counted to ten.

In the following silence, the medical examiner cleared his throat. "Ahem. Uh, if you'll excuse me I'm needed over there."

When she got to ten, she opened her eyes to see the ME beating a hasty retreat off to supervise the loading of Libby's body. She turned to Detective Morgan. "You do understand the senator has ordered me to work with you on this case? You also understand I'm in charge?" She paused, forcing him to acknowledge her. She lifted one eyebrow.

"Yes. And yes."

In the course of her two questions, the heat in his eyes blinked out and his indifferent stance shifted to frozen resistance. *Great*, she thought. *How am I supposed to find Libby's murderer with this imbecile hanging around my neck?*

"Stanton is waiting for us at his home in Kalorama," she said. "I'll see you there." She turned on her heel and walked off as calmly as possible to talk to the ME. Behind her, she heard Morgan's steps crunching in the roadside gravel, then the start of a car quickly peeling out onto the highway.

"Damn," she exhaled. Her hands were shaking and her heart banged against her ribs. When he was answering her questions, Jarvis' threat of residence in the backside of hell was all that kept her from cold-cocking Detective Morgan and wiping his snide demeanor right off the map. She drew a deep breath and walked to the ambulance. "Tell me," she asked the ME. "Did you notice anything odd about the body when you first saw it?"

He pursed his lips. "You've seen plenty of corpses, right?"

She nodded, waiting for him to confirm her observations.

"I thought her skin color looked ... not—"

"What you expected?" she added.

"Yeah. Actually, not like anything I've ever seen before."

"How so?"

"Her skin has a peculiar discoloration I can't speculate on. I'll be looking at that closely."

She nodded. Libby's skin looked shadowed, like she was rubbed down with ash. The girl always had such a clear complexion, avoiding the sun. What could paint her whole body in shadow? Was this information connected to the feather? "Thanks." She turned to leave when he stopped her.

"You don't know, do you?" he asked.

"About?"

"Rhys, Detective Morgan."

She didn't care about Detective Morgan's problems. Reluctant, she shrugged. "No, fill me in."

"You bear a striking resemblance to his wife."

"Oh," she answered deadpan. "So? Did she die tragically?" She spun her finger near her head. "Is that why he doesn't play well with others?"

"No. He caught her sleeping with his partner."

She snorted. "Isn't that just what I need."

GIDEON SMITH CAREFULLY TAPPED HIS LATEST CHEMICAL creation into small plastic bags. He measured them carefully to a half gram. "There," he said, sealing the last one. "We have the latest boutique-high known to modern chemistry, thank you, Dr. Lazar." He dropped the collection of bags into another plastic bag and sealed it.

From advertising on the dark web, a customer had placed an order after he supplied the chemical formula for his drug, then a good-faith money drop was made.

Tomorrow he would send the product and receive the full purchase price in a deposit to a foreign account. It was only five thousand dollars, but it was a good beginning to his boutique drug career.

He chuckled, knowing holier-than-thou Dr. Anthony Lazar would pitch a fit if he knew a sample of his precious Nobility drug had escaped the lab on Draco Station. The space station was kept top secret so billionaire Aaron Monk and his corporate partners in crime could continue to rake in their obscene profits harvesting Vulkillium from the surface of Draco Prime.

"Draco Prime. What a hell hole."

The 'Draco Dragons' created to work on Draco Prime's surface by Lazar in his genetic experiments were the backbone of Pantheon's highly lucrative Draco Station. Creating shifters for working the surface was legal; allowing them to return to earth was not. As long as the volatile operation and Draco Station remained top-secret, the station's wild-west production for the rich and richer by using the poor and poorest would continue without moral oversight.

"It's all about money and power."

He paused, unable to forget last night's horror when he

found Libby dead on the floor. He shivered, thankful she had touched the globe first—otherwise it could have been him dead on the floor.

Still, her death had brought him a heightened sense of protocol. He could not afford any more murders; he was lucky to have gotten away with two.

He packaged the double sealed bags in another bag and repeated the process, making sure there was no DNA or finger prints on the packages. This went into a heavy plain brown envelope with a preprinted address label. Once the label was scanned, he would receive half his money, the other half when the package was picked up and opened.

Easy peezy, lemon squeezy, thanks to Dr. Lazar.

His first couture drug was a combination of cathinones for euphoria with a tweak on the end using the Nobility base Lazar created. Gideon always thought Lazar was crazy to tinker with human DNA, but the Doc was a chemistry genius.

"From Draco Station to the party circuit, get ready for an out of this world high."

3

Dreya pulled up to Senator Stanton's home, hoping to get this interview over without drawing any blood. Seeing Morgan's car in the driveway inside the Secret Service cordon, she parked at the curb and showed her belt badge before being allowed in.

Senator Sanford Stanton paced back and forth in the sitting room of his two-story mansion. She entered the room and immediately tilted her head and squinted.

Something's not right about this picture.

"Dreya," the senator called, seeing her in the doorway. He hurried over and ushered her into the room. "What happened to my daughter?" He drew her to a couch and sat, holding her hand. "What do you know? Who did this to Libby?"

Dreya's suspicions were fast developing. She twitched her nose, smelling not only scotch, but also the political drama. "We don't know yet, sir. What can you tell us about Libby's activities, her whereabouts yesterday?"

"Got it," Detective Morgan said. He walked over and offered her his cell phone.

She took the phone, particularly noting the loss of Morgan's surly attitude. "Thank you." The cell phone displayed a popular celebrity-sighting web page; Morgan had cued up a video. She watched as Libby tossed a drink in a young man's face.

Drama. It's a Stanton family obsession.

She handed the phone back to Morgan, asking the senator, "Can you give us his name, sir?"

Senator Stanton rose, his closed face signaling his loss of interest. "See my PR people. They keep track of all that." He buttoned his jacket and brushed at his pants. "You and Rhys find who did this, understand? Now, if you will excuse me, I have a meeting."

She stood. While they had not confirmed Libby's demise as a murder, she felt certain the girl did not commit suicide, nor did she accidentally fall into the river. "Your daughter was just murdered; won't you take the day off to mourn her?" She couldn't keep the challenge from her words. Her vocal chords rang with indignation for Libby, gone and apparently already dismissed.

He stopped and drilled her with a hard look. "It's been some time since you worked here, Dreya, but little has changed. You know Libby always had a propensity for risky situations. Hell, you saved her life once already. I trust between you and Rhys, you'll find us closure on this ugly matter."

Once he left the room, she exhaled in a huff. "Little has changed, that's for sure." She glanced at Morgan. "Problem?"

He watched her with a wrinkled brow and a piercing gaze. Protesting her words with hands raised in innocence, he pulled his chin back. "No, no problem." He cleared his throat. "Where to now?"

While he looked cool enough, she saw the vein popping in his forehead. She wondered what the senator said to him before she arrived. "We go talk to the boyfriend."

"I'll get his address from the PR people."

"Meet you out front."

Outside the mansion, the area was cleared with Stanton and his detail gone. She walked to her car, tapping her keys against her thigh.

What could have happened to Libby? What could cause a feather to grow and leave behind a shadow in her skin?

She frowned, unable, even in her vivid imagination to concoct a scenario to fit her evidence. Morgan came out and passed her a slip of paper. "The address. See you there."

"Hey," she said. "Are we going to use separate cars for the whole investigation?"

He looked her up and down. "Depends."

She nodded. "My thoughts exactly. See you there." She climbed in her car.

"Brandon Carlisle, 33rd St, Georgetown," Dreya said. She pulled up to the brick condo, seeing Morgan already waiting for her, leaning, again, on the fender of his car. "He pulls that nonchalant shit just to annoy me. And how did he get here so quick?"

As she walked up, he nodded and pushed off from the car. In a move she immediately suspicioned was meant to deliberately irritate her, he extended his arm and bowed so she could pass in front of him. She exhaled and climbed the few steps at Brandon's front door. As she reached for the doorbell, Morgan reached around her shoulder and beat her to it, pressing the bell. She pulled back and skewered him with a frown, silently proclaiming 'cut it out'.

He shrugged one shoulder, and offered his defense. "Well, what else, then, am I here for?"

She turned back to the door, resisting the urge to peg the detective's shin with the toe of her boot.

The door opened. A disheveled, handsome young man stood before them, mid-twenties with dark hair, no shirt, impressive chest, good abs, pajama bottoms riding his hip bones. He looked her over before glancing at Morgan. "Yes?"

"Dreya Love, FBI." She pulled her jacket back, exposing her badge and gun.

"Detective Rhys Morgan." He flipped open his ID.

The kid's eyes bugged and he ran a hand through his hair. "Whoa. Uh, what can I do for you?" He frowned and looked askance at them. "What's going on? Has something happened?"

"May we come in?" she asked.

He backed up. "Sure, come on in."

They entered his home. She occupied Brandon while Morgan walked around. "Where were you last night between midnight and 1:00 A.M.?"

"Why? What's happened?"

"Where were you?"

He snorted a chuckle. "Ha. You must be the only person in DC who doesn't know. Why? What's happened?"

"Libby Stanton died last night."

His mouth dropped open and he stepped back, a hand splayed across his chest. "Oh, my God, Libby? She broke up with me last night."

"What did you do after the infamous drink-tossing break-up?"

He grabbed his phone and showed her a series of selfies

of him and a pair of young brunette ladies; each photo time stamped from 12:15 to after 2:00 A.M. "We left the club and then came here." He motioned towards the hallway and a bedroom door. "If you want to ask them—"

She gave him back his phone. "That won't be necessary."

Morgan finished his circuit and returned to stand with her. "What time did you arrive at the George?"

"We had just gotten there, right about midnight, and ordered our first drink when she flipped out and did her drama queen thing. She doused me with her drink, declaring, 'No one dumps the senator's daughter,' and just walked out."

"Do you know where she was going? Did you see her talk to anyone on the way out?" Morgan asked.

"No, I didn't see anything. I was busy cleaning her drink off my face. At least it was just a Perrier."

"What party drugs did Libby use?" Dreya asked. She glanced at Morgan. He gave a negative shake of his head; he found nothing of interest in his brief walk around.

"She liked to do a little cocaine."

"Did you do coke with her last night?" Morgan asked. He towered over Brandon and peered down at him.

"No." Brandon shook his head, vehement. "No coke last night. We didn't have any and we just got there, the party hadn't started."

"Did you know she was going to break up with you?" Morgan cast a harsh eye at the young man. Dreya wondered what was going through the detective's mind to produce such a dissecting look.

"No." Brandon looked down, grimacing. "Actually, I was going to break it off with her last night, I was just waiting for—"

"Did she have a purse?" she asked.

"Uh, yeah. A black rectangle thing."

Dreya was done; she looked at Morgan. He lifted one brow. She jutted her chin towards the door. Brandon walked with them and reached to open the door, asking, "What happened ... to Libby? How did she—?"

She heard the concern in his voice, but, as with the senator, it was either too little, too late ... or just convenient. "Don't leave town," she answered.

Outside she waited for Morgan. He approached, hands in his pockets, clearly waiting for her directions.

"The George. Let's look at their security video."

"My thoughts," he agreed.

"See you there."

She managed to reach the George before Morgan. "Stop that," she reprimanded herself, calling out her competitive nature. She got out of her car and walked to the sidewalk. Across the street was a parking lot; she saw no visible security cameras.

A car pulled into the drive for the underground parking, and the driver called out. Not recognizing him, she looked around. Morgan was sitting behind her on a brick retaining wall around a restaurant patio.

How does he do that?

He waved to the driver and rose, joining her. "That's the head of security. I called him up, told him we need to see the camera footage."

She resisted asking him how he got here so fast, instead silently appreciating his detective work. That he knew the security man was not a surprise; such was the value of local boots on the ground.

They followed the car down into the basement parking. The driver got out and greeted Morgan with zeal. "Hey, man, how are you doing?"

Morgan complied with an elaborate handshake, saying, "Wesley my man, life is good. You look like the George is treating you well."

While they completed their ritual, she waited. Wesley shot a glance at her and whispered into Morgan's ear. Morgan shook his head emphatically. Wesley whispered more until Morgan then nodded in agreement. Wesley came away, smiling broadly.

"Agent Love, this is Wesley, head of security."

She offered the effervescent Wesley her hand. "Thanks for meeting us here so quickly," she said, grateful for the moment he finally released her.

He winked. "Any time you want in the George, just mention my name."

"Thank you, Wesley. I'll keep that in mind." A quick look at Morgan showed his face had retreated into his scowl.

Huh, she thought. Mercurial.

Wesley had opened a door to a security closet in the garage and was cueing up the video. "Midnight you say?"

"Start a little earlier—11:30," she said.

They perused the video over Wesley's shoulder. As the cars sped by, she watched for Brandon's red BMW. "There," she pointed. "Stop." The red vehicle clearly stood out; she could see Libby's image in the passenger seat, time stamp at 11:49. "Go ahead."

The video started back up. People and cars coming and going. "There she is," Morgan said. "Stop it."

Libby walked out to the sidewalk. She looked at her watch, then drew her phone out of her black purse. "Looking for another party?" Dreya mused. "Or getting an Uber ride home?" She checked the time—12:10.

A car pulled to the curb. Libby spoke with someone in

the vehicle; she still has her phone in her hand. "Can you get another view?" she asked. "I can't see anything."

Libby chatted with the unseen driver for a couple of minutes. At 12:15 she put her phone back in her purse and got into the car. The vehicle pulled out without a view of the driver or the license plate.

"What you see is what you get," Wesley said. "I only have this one camera outside." He peered closely at the image on the screen. "Libby Stanton. Something happen to her?"

"Forget we were here, Wesley," Morgan said. His tone was less congenial, more authoritative. "Understand?"

"Uh, sure, man. You need anything else?"

"No. Go home."

Dreya walked out front to the sidewalk and stared at the street. "What happened to you, Libby? Where did you go? Why did you get into the car with this man? Was he a stranger? Or someone you knew? Which direction did you go?"

Morgan joined her. "So, at 12:15 she gets into an unknown vehicle." He faced west. "The only traffic cams west of Wisconsin are on M Street, so unless they went down M, we've lost her. East, on the other hand—"

Her phone buzzed, stopping him. "Huh," she grunted. "That's quick. Assistant ME Bailey wants to see us." She slipped the phone in her jacket pocket. "See you there, Morgan."

He gave her a sharp look under heavy brows, and exhaled, as if relenting to a task he dreaded. "Yeah. See you there, Love."

Transformation

AT THE FORENSICS LAB, DREYA ENTERED THE OUTER OFFICE TO the autopsy room. Unless there was a necessity, she preferred not to view Libby's autopsied body on the table. She sat, waiting for Morgan to show, remembering the first time she met Libby.

Dreya was fresh out of the Navy and considering her future. Because of her top military clearance, she was hired for private security and ended up on the senator's in-house detail assigned to his then teenage daughter. At seventeen that summer, Libby was a loose cannon targeting her father's political career.

"He only cares about me when it serves his purposes," Libby complained. She was sitting with her feet in the pool at 1:00 A.M., a bottle of tequila in her hand.

A seasoned drinker in her own right, Dreya remembered how the seventeen-year-old drank the potent tequila with eye-watering abandon. She tried to ease the bottle away from the girl. Having none of that, Libby pouted and clutched her tequila to her chest. "My bottle. Get your own."

Dreya took her shoes off and rolled her pants up. She sat next to Libby with her feet in the warm water. "Don't you think you're being a little hard on your father?"

Libby pursed her lips with a 'puff' of disdain and a wave of her hand. "The senator has more important things to do ... like saving the world."

She took a drink from the bottle and wiped her mouth on her shirt sleeve. She turned on Dreya, her eyes suddenly bright above a guess-what-I-know grin. "You should hear some of the things they talk about." She lowered her voice and darted a glance right and left. "It's out of this world stuff my daddy does. Out of this world."

Libby got to her feet with amazing grace considering how empty the tequila bottle was. "Daddy," she said with a sneer, "only has time for important feathers." She swung the bottle with drunken emphasis. "Feathers are important—not daughters." She straightened and handed the bottle to Dreya. "Here, I'm going to bed." She remained weaving on her feet as Dreya stood and put her shoes back on.

"I like you," Libby blurted before she ambled off.

Dreya kept up with Libby, watching to make sure she made it to her bed without breaking anything. Obviously an experienced drunk, the teen managed to reach her bed and pass out fully clothed without puking. Dreya put a trash can by the bed just in case.

"Good night," she said, closing the bedroom door. She stayed there for some time, listening to see if Libby needed help. She snorted with the irony. How many times did she perform this task, this follow-the-drunk routine for her inebriated mother. "Well, you never know what life's preparing you for."

When she finally walked away that night, she wondered what word Libby was trying for in her intoxicated state when she said 'feathers'. At the time, she thought it was just the ramblings of a pickled brain, but sitting in the ME's office, knowing Libby was sliced open in the next room, she had to wonder ... if feathers is the word Libby intended, what the hell was she talking about?

A pair of men's voices pulled her from her reverie. Astonished, she saw Morgan walk out of the autopsy theater, chatting with the ME. Standing, she squinted at the detective, tilting her head.

How the hell does he do that?

Bailey returned to the autopsy room while Morgan walked over to her, shaking his head. She swallowed her amazement at him beating her from location to location. She was annoyed, yet perversely grateful, for his timing kept her from having to enter the autopsy room with Libby on the table. He drew out his notepad and went down his list.

"Bailey didn't have a whole lot," he reported. "With it still being a little early, we're filling in the 'rule out' list. Libby's stomach contents were benign; she was not pregnant; had no evidence of sexual activity or assault; and no evidence of drug use via injection or snorting that evening; and there were no fingerprints on her body. The nail clippings will take a day or two."

She waited for him to mention—

"The ME did say her skin color anomaly was not restricted to just her skin."

She frowned, trying to unravel that statement.

"Apparently, the color anomaly is across the board. He has slides of various tissues, and the anomaly is consistent in muscle, skin, and organs. He doesn't know, yet, the cause of this."

She pinched the bridge of her nose. "And we won't get the toxicology report for weeks."

A color anomaly. A feather. What the hell is going on?

"Let's go to her apartment," she said. "P Street, North West. I'll see you there."

She knew the way. The P Street residence was a family property Libby inherited when she collected her Political Science degree from Georgetown University last year. Dreya attended a small post-graduation celebration there.

Libby was so bright and animated, proud of her degree. She waited for her father to come, but as the hour grew later, her cheer faded. When it became clear he wasn't going to show, she opened a bottle of tequila and poured a stiff portion into a glass. She tipped the glass to Dreya and said, "Told you—and I was right, wasn't I?"

Pushing the memory aside, Dreya declared, "Libby,

honey, you were a victim from birth." She pulled into a parking spot out front and reluctantly smiled, seeing Morgan already here.

He met her on the walk. "Ready?" He flashed a key.

"How did you get that?"

"The senator's PR people."

He walked ahead and opened the door, approached the alarm box and tapped in the code. She pulled on gloves. He took the living room and kitchen; she went through the bedroom and bath.

She ran her hands under the edge of the mattress; rifled the bedside stand and found a sex toy, some condoms, and an erotic novel. She went to her knees and passed her flashlight under the bed. Nothing under there, but she found several used condoms in the bedside trash. She bagged and tagged them for evidence.

In the bathroom, the medicine cabinet provided nothing pharmaceutical. An array of cosmetics and skin care products littered the counter; all were high dollar, nothing from a drugstore.

In the front room, Morgan was finishing up. "It's clean. The bar is well stocked with only the best."

"No phone?"

"No phone."

"We'll need a warrant for the server, then."

"And we need to search traffic cams," he added.

She pulled out her phone. "I'll call the senator. With nothing on this end, we'll have to go back to the beginning."

Morgan stopped her. "Wait. I have a buddy over in Traffic Division. I'll go take a look at the traffic cam footage. You write up the server warrant and go home. We can't do anything else until tomorrow when we access the server.

Let's see if anything else pops before hitting up the senator again."

He was right. He was also very efficient. She understood why the senator wanted him on the case. She looked at her watch. It was just noon. What a long morning this has been.

This gives me time to spend the afternoon with Kit.

"All right," she said. "I'll see you in the morning ... somewhere."

"Count on it," he said.

4

Rhys Morgan settled in to his desk at the Metro PD office. He typed a name and sent the background search humming through the databases available to him, seeking out any details concerning the life of Special Agent Dreya Michelle Love.

He hummed and tapped his fingers on the desk. His new 'partner' was an enigma wrapped in a puzzle he wanted to unravel. She was a challenge not only to his sensibilities, but to the status quo in more ways than one. He wasn't averse to her challenging his sensibilities, but disrupting the status quo was not going to happen.

When he saw her at the crime scene, she did, at first glance, have a glaring resemblance to Joanie, his soon-to-be ex-wife. The truth, however, is Joanie never looked so good. Certainly, the initial resemblance was there; hell, they could be sisters. But Agent Love's skin, her smoky green eyes, and that mass of hair—

"Stop what you're doing," he demanded. He exhaled and looked away from the computer, grateful for the absence of the mid-week crush of office personnel. He didn't need a nosey audience today.

Agent Love is hot; I need to keep her at arm's distance.

"Maybe," he mumbled and shrugged one shoulder. The fact that she was entirely desirable was in contradiction to him acknowledging—

She's an authority unto herself.

"Good point," he said, "for that spells trouble. But why is the Special Agent so ... special? What sets you apart, Dreya Love?"

Knowing the background search would take some time, he made a call to Traffic Division. "Hey, Robert, it's Morgan. I need to look at some traffic cam footage from Saturday night, between midnight and 1:00 A.M. Yep. I'm on my way."

Two hours later he returned from Traffic Division to his desk. "Just as I thought, a waste of my Sunday afternoon," he grumbled. He checked his incoming messages and saw his background search on Agent Love arrived. "All right now, let's see what makes Miss Love tick, because she definitely ... ticks."

Like a bomb.

He scanned through the entries. "Hmm, overachiever. A Criminal Justice degree from Virginia Commonwealth University." His eyebrows shot up over the next entry.

"Six years in the Navy, 03 Lieutenant, Expert Rifle, Expert Pistol, Afghanistan, Iraq, Bronze Star, Purple Heart—holy shit."

Before reading on, he had to sit back a moment to consider just how badass his 'partner' was. "Ah, here's the senator, that's how she knows the family, did a year of in-house security for the daughter." He sucked at his teeth. "Loosing someone you know like that is harsh. She went to Quantico at age 29, moved up rather quickly until—"

"Uh oh." Suddenly the lines of department speak required translating. "So, she turned in her partner for corruption, oh my." Seeing all he needed, he deleted the file and leaned back, thinking.

Tough on the outside, soft on the inside. That's a dangerous combination in this line of work. He checked his watch and drummed his fingers on the desk, deciding it was early enough to cruise by the agent's apartment—just to see what there is to see.

He parked a block off from Love's place in Arlington. Seeing her dated Audi parked on the street, he settled back to see what the agent did on her afternoon off. Her official personal history indicated one thing.

Let's see if she walks what she talks.

She set a high bar on all points, physically, intellectually, professionally, morally. "Hmm. Something in there going to break one day." In response, an unbidden thought from the deep sprang up ...

Sounds familiar.

"Huh," he complained. "Don't be so quick. The fat lady hasn't set foot on stage yet." A taxi pulled up to Love's home. She came out the front door and greeted a teenage girl, paid the driver, and she and the girl went inside.

"Hmm, not a relative; the girl has black hair." He sat up and watched her windows through his binoculars. At this angle and distance, there was little to see. Soon, they came out and got in the Audi, laughing and having a good time. The Audi pulled out; he followed a block behind, keeping at least six cars between them.

They traveled east and crossed the river, ending up in a boutique area on Pennsylvania NW. He parked, still a block away, and used his binoculars, watching as they got out of the car and entered a bookstore. "Huh. They certainly are congenial."

They were in the bookstore for over an hour and came out with the girl carrying a bag. Still smiling and laughing, they walked a short distance to an ice cream shop, went in and came out with huge cones piled with ice cream. They occupied a little table out front for a half hour, enjoying the summer afternoon and devouring the cones. The sight of Agent Love's lips slurping up the melting treat made Rhys uncomfortable.

He watched as they finished their cones and returned to the Audi. Back at Love's home, another taxi showed up for the girl. Agent Love stood on the sidewalk, waving as the taxi left. She went in and the lights came on.

Rhys remained at his vantage point.

His day began with the Libby Stanton murder phone call at 5:05 A.M. Agent Love showed up with personal history with the victim. Then there was Senator Stanton. Rhys recalled the senator's words, "Work with Dreya; find whoever did this to my daughter. But report to me privately. Understand?"

Rhys understood all right. He understood senators do pretty much what they want without paying the bill—there was always an underling to handle any messy details. As with most people with great power, the senator this morning managed to make Rhys feel like an underling.

"Why does he want me to report to him?"

He's afraid of something sticking to his ass, and I'm the toilet paper.

"Huh," he grunted.

Now we have the ever so impressive Agent Love. She didn't strike him as a piece of toilet paper. She's more like a rock in your shoe kind of girl, immutable in her own right. And Stanton knows that.

He wants me to backdoor Love's investigation. Why?

First, the senator suspects the situation can give him vulnerability of the worst kind—political exposure. Rhys had worked this town a long time and knew there were countless bodies buried like landmines, waiting for their explosive moment in the fifteen-minute news cycle. His shoulders twitched with revulsion, thinking about the kind of secrets bartered daily in the District. He was personally galled to think the senator felt he held moral ground over him.

Second, and most offensive, the senator believed Rhys had his back. He started his car. "Well, that's his mistake."

A mistake men of power often make.

AFTER A FUN AFTERNOON WITH KIT, HER TEENAGE MENTEE, Dreya relaxed on her couch, setting a cup of tea on the side table. In her hand was a freshly printed personnel file on Detective Rhys Morgan.

"Hmm." She thumbed through the papers. "Looks pretty standard. No military service. Rose to Detective Third Grade; four years in Robbery/Homicide; almost lost his badge over authority issues; moved to DC Homicide Desk before retiring. Retired? Huh," she snorted. "But returned to DC Cold Case Squad, then over to Special Detective."

Everything she'd seen of Rhys Morgan told her the detective was a far more complicated package than the file in her hands revealed. His history indicated he had rather pronounced ethical borders.

"So do I, until they start preventing me from solving or

preventing a crime." While he had been helpful to her so far, she really didn't want or need his help going forward. She had her own methods he might object to.

I can't have Detective Morgan's compunctions getting in my way; I have my own compunctions to massage.

"I'll just have to work around him. Let him drive his own car; that keeps him out of my hair."

Remember, you have to work with him.

"Pfft," she snorted.

No matter what it took, she would find out what happened to Libby, senator or not, Rhys Morgan or not. She opened a box on the side table and removed the evidence bag containing Libby's feather. She examined it closely in the light of a table lamp. There was a faint iridescence on the tiny soft down at the base of the feather; it was pearlescent and quite beautiful.

She taped on her tablet and searched the internet for a few information websites that were little more than freak shows. What she understood is while many objects that look like feathers can come from the human body, it's not possible to produce them naturally.

Humans can't grow feathers; we don't have the DNA.

"So how and why would a feather be growing from Libby's chest? How did she acquire the DNA?" She stared at the feather, letting her mind wander through her options. The important question was, "Do I show this little beauty to Morgan?"

The evidence bag went back in the box. "I think not."

The next morning, she rose early, intending to get a head start on Morgan and meet him at her office, assuming he had the sense to show up there. His lofty sense of autonomy irritated her, even as she acknowledged the similarity to her own independent nature.

She opened the door to leave and found Morgan on her doorstep. "Oh. It's you," she blurted.

Damn.

"Do you need something, Detective Morgan?"

"Let's talk," he said and walked in.

She closed the door behind him and watched as he sat on the couch, forcing herself not to look at the box containing the feather just inches from his hand. Crossing her arms, she asked, "You have something on your mind?" She remained standing by the door.

"Yes," he said.

Today his handsome face was animated with a rather engaging expression. Ignoring his demeanor, she remained like a monolith with her well-practiced deadpan look.

Engage this, sucker.

"We have a rather delicate situation," he said. "Stanton is going to expect a lot from us." He cleared his throat. "I'm not sure what all that might include."

She refused to respond.

Is he admitting to being compromised by the senator?

Not clear if she fully understood his point, she nodded encouragement.

"And since you know the senator, now would be a good time for any disclosure you might be ... holding back."

One of her eyebrows shot up momentarily at his insinuation she had something to disclose. She looked down and fixed her expression, annoyed he had gotten to her. She shifted on her feet before looking up, reading his body language.

His posture indicated he was open and receptive. Conversely, she noted herself standing with arms crossed, glaring down at him. She exhaled and dropped her arms.

"What are you suggesting?" She sat in the chair by the couch.

"Is there anything with the family ... or the senator's business dealings you consider to have a bearing on this case? As of now we're at zero."

She relaxed, realizing he was not accusing her, he was simply asking for deep information she might have on the family. "I agree about us having zero. As for the senator, the family is predictably political and dysfunctional. Stanton is what you saw yesterday—politics and power are his family. Sadly, Libby was just something that happened along the way to the senate. As remote as kidnapping-gone-bad might be, we'll have to consider it."

"The senator didn't seem concerned in that direction," he added. "But he does have the expectation we'll figure out what happened to his daughter."

She rose and began pacing. "Libby got in a car with someone and drove off. Within an hour, she was dead."

Morgan stood and walked to an open area in the dining space adjacent to where she paced. He pushed his hands in his pockets and leaned against the counter while she continued back and forth. She asked, "Do we feel it worth looking into other clubs that night?"

"Given the short time span between the last sight of her and her death, I doubt it, but we should keep that open. Go back to the boyfriend?"

"No," she said. "He's not our guy, his alibi is solid and well documented." She exhaled with frustration. "And there's no help yet from the ME's office."

"Bailey's going to call me if anything comes up," Morgan said. "He's looking into the discoloration thing."

She stopped, fists propped on her hips. "I'd like to get my hands on her phone. I checked out her Facebook page; she was a big selfie fan. If she took a picture and sent it out, it'll be on the server. Calls to her number are going right to voicemail. I searched for her phone last night and got nothing. The senator used to track her with the GPS; she got smart and learned how to disable it."

"The search warrant for the server should pop by this morning," he said.

"So, Libby just disappears off the face of the planet, dies, and turns up dead in the river. The only thing missing in our timeline is her murder."

They came face to face.

Lips pinched, she cocked her head and squinted. "Who is that man in the car?"

"Where did they go?" he added. "What did he give her to cause the coloration anomaly?"

His question fired her next one. "Where did he get whatever it is he gave her?"

Their brainstorming played off one another.

"Is he a drug dealer?"

She answered quickly. "No. She had high standards."

"A professional partier, one of her friends on the circuit with a bad batch?"

"He'd have to be smooth—"

"Educated—"

"Good looking—"

"Well dressed—"

"Near her age—"

"Nice car—"

Their back and forth banter came to an abrupt stop.

"That's half of DC."

Their explosive energy fizzled. He leaned back against the counter, replacing his hands in his pockets and staring at his shoes. She gazed out the window, her lips twitched to one side. "Yep. Still got nothing," she said.

"I can talk to the DEA," he offered. "See if anything similar is out on the street. I doubt it though. The ME would alert us if anything related was coming through the morgue."

"I'll put up a watch notice on Interpol."

A silence filled the room, one of determination sparing with frustration.

"I was afraid of that," he murmured.

"Yeah, me, too. Back to the senator?"

"Back to the senator."

She grabbed her keys and locked up, meeting him on the sidewalk. He waited for her; an air of expectation lifted one corner of his mouth.

"Yes?" she asked, stopping abruptly.

"I thought I'd drive ... us, if you think you'll feel safe with me behind the wheel."

She would have snorted with disbelief, but he was watching her closely. While she wanted to split up, to do so in the face of him offering to drive would draw attention, the very thing she didn't need.

Damn. Got that one wrong.

"Sure," she said. At least now, she thought, *I can see how you got everywhere first.* But he drove like a normal, law abiding driver, taking no extreme measures or routes. They traveled and arrived exactly as they would have had she been behind the wheel. She got out, making note of the mystery behind his driving.

In her office, the results of the server search warrant were in. She combed through the lines before passing the pages to him. "There was no activity on her phone from the time she reached the George until the time of her death. No calls, no texts, no emails. Zip, dammit, nada, zilch."

She sat on her desk next to him, realizing she was not only stuck with him, but she had zero on this case. "Shall we go see the senator?" She pulled her shades out of her pocket. "You're driving."

5

On the way to the Stanton home, Dreya's thoughts were interrupted.

"So, what are you thinking?" Morgan asked.

"Nothing. You know. Maybe just my restless gut."

"So, what's making your gut restless?"

Suddenly, she regretted her decision to ride with him. "What are you? A pest?" She pulled back to glare at him.

"No," he said smoothly as he drove. "I'm just a good detective and I see the wheels turning in my partner's head. I want to know what's going on. That's all. My shot with the senator is the old corporate/political enemies angle. You have something different, don't you?"

She looked out the window. He referred to her as his partner, a title she wasn't sure she wanted. Accepting the title, even informally, would mean having to show him the feather, and she wasn't sure the time was right for such a twofold revelation—that she had the evidence and that she kept it from him. Hell, she wasn't sure how the feather was pertinent to the case. "My gut," she said, answering him, "is just restless for evidence."

They reached the senator's home without any more probing from the detective. Dreya followed him in and let him do the talking once they reached the upstairs office. She walked around the room, eyeing the many photographs adorning the office walls. Behind her, Morgan did his best to evade the pitfalls of interviewing a senator.

"Sir, we've little in the way of suspects at the moment—"

She kept herself from cringing, glad she wasn't able to see the upcoming steel in Stanton's next words as they pierced the detective.

"Then why are you here, Detective?"

With her face out of view, she grimaced. Cold shot to the center mass. Senator one. Detective zero.

"Because our next suspect pool will come from your acquaintances, sir."

Oh, bravo! Point goes to the detective. She stepped over to the next wall and assumed the innocent stance of a bystander. This gave her a peripheral view of the confrontation.

Senator Stanton puffed up, drawing all the air from the room. "Are you suggesting—?"

Oops, she thought. Game playing strategy, Morgan, time to back down.

"Of course, we're not suggesting anything, sir. We are trying to find your daughter's murderer, who is still at large. With a shortage of suspects from her social life—" He paused before continuing.

Uh oh, wrong thing to admit, she thought. She maintained her uninvolved facade and stepped to another row of photos.

Morgan finished with a tactic he deployed well—deliberately poking the bear. "We are considering the possibility of a professional."

Nicely played. She looked down, hiding her grin, waiting for the senator's response. She could hear him considering what to say, eternally gauging the world stage which is always a video away. His next words confirmed she had read him accurately.

"Do you think I'm in danger?"

She was glad she wasn't Morgan, glad she didn't have to present a professional demeanor in the face of such unmitigated cowardice.

"No sir, we would have notified the Secret Service if we had a suspect or felt you were in direct danger. But can you think of anyone who would wish you or your daughter harm?"

Dreya turned around, wanting to personally observe the senator as he lied.

"Why, no, of course not," Stanton protested. "Everybody loves me, except for a few across the aisle."

"Any business enemies due to your political position?"

Stanton shrugged off the notion. "All politicians have dissidents." He peered over Morgan's shoulder and caught Dreya's eye. "Are you sure I'm under no threat?"

No threat of genuine family responsibility or moral excess, she thought. "No, sir. You're not in any danger we're aware of."

"What large corporations or lobbies have you butted heads with lately?" Morgan asked.

Stanton brought his attention back to the detective. "None," he answered hesitantly.

He was obviously choosing his words. She peered at him, wishing she could crack his head open and pry out what he knew. Then again, she quickly decided she didn't want anything from the senator's head becoming part of her world.

"Any of the aforementioned," Morgan persisted, "that have profited from your alliance?"

"Again, are you suggesting—?"

"Suggesting nothing, just trying to see all sides and players on the board." Morgan had relaxed his posture and placed his hands in his pockets in the good 'ol boy stance. He cocked his head and shrugged one shoulder. "We want to find your daughter's killer, sir. That requires a little poking and some questions here and there. You know how it is."

Stanton narrowed his eyes and pursed his lips. Knowing the expression well, she braced herself for a Stanton edict.

"I'm leaving within the hour on a three day mission overseas," he stated. "A mission that should have been six days." He skewered her with a look. "A mission I cut short to come home for my daughter's funeral service."

A bolt of laughter threatened to erupt from her chest. She looked down, knowing in her heart there was a special place in hell for fathers like Sanford Stanton.

"And when I return," he continued, "I expect to have the news that you have identified and captured my daughter's murderer."

Because, she thought, there must be a press conference after the service ...

Stanton's words confirmed her suspicions. He drew himself up with a flash of momentary grief as questionable as his scruples. "I'm having a small press release after the service. Make certain I have news that will make us all look good, Detective, Agent. Now, please excuse me, I have to go."

She joined Morgan as they walked out the door. Once they drove a half block down the street, he said, "This guy is so dirty."

"Yeah, but is he connected to his daughter's death?"

His face looked grim. "He's connected to everything somehow, someway."

"In his office, one thing I saw he was connected to is Phillip Taylor of the Pantheon Group."

"Pantheon. They're one of those multi-national, inter-continental—"

"Global and beyond," she said. "I read it from one of the award photos Stanton has on the wall."

"What does that mean?"

"Exactly."

Before he could park, her phone buzzed. So did his. "It's a notice to come see something over at Forensics," she said.

At the lab, they were met by Assistant Medical Examiner Bailey. "A rug washed up on shore. We think Libby was wrapped in it when she entered the river."

They followed him into the lab where an eight by five area rug was rolled out. Caught in one of the loops of the fringe was a stiletto heel minus the rest of the shoe. It matched the single shoe Libby was wearing.

"I compared the heel to the one Libby was wearing; it's a match," Bailey said.

"This definitely ties her to the rug," Morgan said. "So, where did the rug come from?"

She looked close. "Looks new, but cheap, maybe a discount store."

He offered other options. "Yard sale, resale shop, dumpster diving."

The ME put on gloves and extracted the heel from the rug fringe, placing it on a steel tray. He pulled the corner of the rug over with his forceps. On the backside was a barcode sticker. "Perhaps this will help."

"Finally, a break," she said.

Morgan looked down his nose from his lofty height and shook his head. "Wouldn't hold my breath on that one."

Within a few minutes the lab had a copy of the bar code and was running it through their master database. While they waited, she began pacing, running through the night of Libby's murder. "You pick up a girl from the club and take her home."

Morgan chimed in. "Somehow, the girl dies."

"Why not just call the police?" she challenged.

"You're hiding something," he offered. "You have a secret, you don't want the authorities poking around in your life. Can't call."

The play-by-play was gaining speed. "So, you have to get rid of the body. Maybe you didn't kill her, maybe it's an accident. But the body has to go somewhere."

"It's 1:00 A.M.," he continues. "You think of the river. But you need something to disguise the body."

"A rug, of course, because you're an amateur."

"And because a rug works."

She went back to her pacing. "You're smart enough not to buy this rug a block from where you live. You drive out of town, somewhere rural, but open all night."

"You have a garage. You need cover to load the body in the trunk of the car."

"You drive to Anacostia Park. It's late at night, no one cares what they see over there."

"Okay," Morgan said. "That's how the senator's daughter got dumped. Now if we can find a little evidence to support this tale ... you know, evidence, that thing we build cases on."

She cocked one eyebrow. "This rug is our break, I feel it."

"I thought your gut had a feeling about the senator."

Imitating him, she lifted her nose. "It does. I can have more than one suspect in my sights."

The technician tapped the counter. "Got it. The rug is from a Store Mart in Falls Church." He printed out the product data page and passed it to Morgan. "Enjoy the drive."

Dreya rubbed her hands together. Finally, something to work with. "I told you we were getting a break."

The drive out to Falls Church was quiet. Her head was filled with a circle having no end, no beginning. Considering Libby's death an accident would have been a relief, except for the oddities concerning her body.

The skin color anomaly, and the feather.

"I got a really bad feeling about this one, Morgan."

He pulled into the parking lot of the Store Mart, slowly driving around looking for security cameras. She noted several busted parking lot lights and not many cameras; what few she saw were all aimed at the front doors. They parked and got out. He looked over the top of the car, at last responding to her comment. "Yep. I do, too. Got a really bad feeling."

Inside, they showed their ID and spoke with the store manager, Mr. Hollingsworth. "We have in-store cameras covering the checker's stations and the front door," he said. "Unfortunately, most of the parking lot cams are non-operational. We're an off-the-main store with a limited budget for these things." He pulled up a section of the footage. "This is from Saturday night, after midnight."

Two cashiers were open. The level of traffic was dismal. One cashier sat on a stool with a book in her hands when the man with the rug walked up to her register. "There," Dreya pointed. "Stop the camera."

She and Morgan leaned closer to the screen. The image

was grainy and poorly focused. A man placed the rolled-up rug sealed in heavy plastic wrap on the counter. The cashier scanned it, the man pulled money from his wallet. Change was delivered with the receipt—the transaction was complete.

"Can you see anything?" Morgan muttered under his breath.

She could see very little. She could hear even less. "We need to speak with this cashier," she told the manager.

"That's Janice, and she should be here shortly. She usually works the eight to four, but she's picking up a shift for someone on vacation."

"We'll wait," she said. With Morgan trailing, she went back to the rug department and walked around the surrounding aisles. "This is our guy."

They stopped, arms crossed, and stared at the vertical stack of rolled and plastic wrapped rugs, as if waiting for the next show to begin. "He was here," she said. "We could pull fingerprints from these wrapped rugs."

Morgan shifted his stance and stuffed his hands in his pockets. "Or, he may have just grabbed one of the five by eights because he wasn't shopping for a rug, he just needed a five by eight."

He was reminding her she was reaching. She huffed with frustration.

Well, when I reach, I usually get something.

"Let's go talk to Janice."

The girl was waiting for them in the manager's office. She was early twenties, thin, pretty, likely a student. Dreya sat in a folding chair next to her, while Morgan lounged in the background. Mr. Hollingsworth sat behind his desk. "Janice, do you remember this sale Saturday night?" He cued the footage of the rug transaction on the monitor.

"Oh, yeah, the guy with the rug. He was cute."

The video paused at the point of her handing him the change. Dreya asked, "What did you say to him here, when he took his change?"

"I told him he could bring it back if he didn't like it."

"Why did you mention the return policy?" she asked.

"Because the rug was cheap and cheesy, not his style at all. Maybe it was a gift for someone else; it certainly wasn't for him."

"Did he say anything?" Morgan asked.

"No, he just nodded. He was very polite. Cute like I said, if a little overdressed. He looked and acted like he had money, obviously educated."

"Any other impression you could tell us?" Dreya probed.

Janice tipped her head, lips pursed, eyes drifting with memory. She snapped back to the present. "Smooth. All things considered—the clothes, the look, his voice ... what little I heard—he was definitely smooth."

"Thank you, Janice," Dreya said. "We appreciate your help."

Janice rose and moved towards the door. "What did he do?"

Dreya knew the question was coming. The innocent always asked. The truth was, they really didn't want to know how close their lives intersected with murderers, rapists, serial killers and madmen. "We don't know anything for sure yet," she answered.

When Janice left, Morgan asked the manager, "Do you have any footage from the parking lot?"

Mr. Hollingsworth shook his head. "It would just cover him exiting the door. Nothing I have reaches into the parking lot. Sorry."

"Thanks. We appreciate your help."

Outside the store's entrance, Dreya paused for Morgan while he made a phone call. She rolled her shoulders and squeezed her left trap with her fingers to relieve the tightness. Morgan put his phone in his jacket pocket and motioned her over. "Come on." His eyes were bright and a smile graced his lips. "My buddy in Traffic is pulling footage for us and sending it to your office."

Slightly less enthusiastic, she mused. "Dark, late model sedans leaving Arlington and entering the District between 3:00 and 4:00 A.M." She didn't have the same bright eyes he had over this one. Her thoughts echoed his earlier dim prediction, 'Wouldn't hold my breath on that one' about the barcode on the rug. But he had been wrong about the barcode, maybe she was wrong about this.

He apparently had his own gut feeling about this lead as he turned on his lights and pushed the speed limit until they crossed the river.

In her office, the footage was waiting. The two of them gazed at the yellow lit street corners of four locations on the monitor. She stared at passing cars until her eyes watered.

He pointed. "There, stop it."

She moved the footage back to follow one sedan. "That's our guy?" The sedan looked like all the others. "What evidence tells you this?"

He nudged her shoulder and grinned. "The car is clean, so it's parked in a garage. It's brand new, and I see a good-sized trunk. That's enough for me. Oh, and I got a gut feeling."

His delivery was dry as last week's toast but his smile was forgiving. She noted his use of her words from earlier about the rug and attempted to muster a level of excitement. Certainly, a name, any name, was better than nothing.

He printed a photo of the car passing through an intersection, clearly displaying the license plate. He typed the numbers into the database. Soon a driver's license with photo and address appeared on the screen.

"Gideon Smith," he read. "Come on. Let's ask Gideon about his poor taste in rugs in the middle of the night."

Smith's address was a ground floor corner townhouse south of Logan Circle. They parked in front of his small plot of grass next to a garage. Morgan scanned the area. "Above my pay grade."

Dreya snorted. "Me, too. What do you bet he's a chemist or pharmacist?"

He opened his car door. "I want to hear what Mr. Gideon did with the rug."

6

Gideon was just getting ready to head out the door for a run when he noticed a man and woman walking up to his door. The woman pointed to his garage, and the movement revealed a gun and badge on her belt.

Cops! What do I do?

Do not go to jail.

He ducked into the bathroom, splashed water at his neck, his armpits, chest and dribbled some down his back. More went on his arms and legs. He grabbed a hand towel and scrubbed his face to make it red, then splashed water on his face and threw the towel around his neck to cover his carotid artery jumping with adrenaline.

The doorbell rang. He looked at his reflection. Satisfied with his appearance, he went to let them in. He opened the door. "Hello."

The tall dark haired man flipped open his credentials. Gideon's heart rate went through the roof.

Approaching Gideon's front door, Dreya pointed to the attached garage.

"Yep," Morgan grunted. He stepped in front of her and rang the doorbell. She let him grandstand, keeping a spot behind him where she unsnapped her gun and cleared her jacket from her holster.

The door opened. A thirty-something man, handsome, brown hair, blue eyes, wearing running clothes, greeted them. "Hello."

Morgan flipped open his credentials. "I'm Detective Morgan."

She stepped out. "I'm Special Agent Love." She made sure he could see her badge and remained standing in the open, watching him. He blotted at his face with the towel.

"What can I help you with, officers?"

"Are you Gideon Smith?" Morgan asked.

"Yes."

"We have a few questions for you, Mr. Smith. May we come in?"

He opened the door, motioning them in. "Excuse me," he said, waving to his appearance. "I just ran."

Dreya held her tongue. Once she got a good look at Smith, she moved him into first position for Libby's unknown man. He was exactly the kind of guy Libby would get in a car with. Now all she had to do was collect enough evidence to make Morgan happy. Unfortunately, Smith displayed no signs of culpability … and his sweaty, red-faced appearance masked any signs of nervousness he might have.

She followed Morgan in. The living room was small but tastefully decorated. A hall went to the right and past two closed doors, likely a bathroom with a bedroom across the way, terminating with a probable main bedroom at the end of the hall.

Smith led them into the kitchen area. "What's this about, officers?"

Morgan made a display of pulling out his notepad and opening it up. He delivered the movement with such suspense, she had to turn away to keep from laughing out loud when he spoke.

"You bought a rug in Falls Church early Sunday morning at 1:56 A.M."

Smith pulled back, surprised. "I did. Is that a crime?"

"No. May we see the rug?"

"As it turns out, I didn't like the rug after all and disposed of it."

"How exactly did you dispose of the rug, sir?"

Comically, Smith asked, "Is rug disposal a crime now?"

"Could be," Morgan replied. "Depends on certain details. When did you dispose of the rug?"

Smith exhaled, looking put out. "That same night after I got home. I opened it up and didn't like it, so I took it to a donation center, you know, the one on—"

She stepped up. "Why didn't you just return it, Mr. Smith? The cashier informed you of the return policy."

"Yes, but the rug was cheap. I bought it on a whim and the thing wasn't worth driving all the way back to Falls Church." He guided them to the front door and opened it.

Morgan stopped and turned to Smith, pen poised over his notepad. "By the way, why were you in Falls Church at 2:00 A.M.?"

"Insomnia. I was driving around to get sleepy."

"Insomnia? Where were you between midnight and 1:30, prior to purchasing the rug?"

"Driving. It was a long night. Is there anything else?"

"No, that's all, Mr. Smith," she answered. She and Morgan stepped out the front door. She looked back, holding her breath, waiting for the question they always have to ask. But he politely nodded bye and closed the door in their faces.

She turned on her heel; Morgan was right behind her. When they were in the car and a block down the street, she said, "It's him. Smith's our guy." She looked at Morgan for his rebuttal.

"What tells you he's our guy—besides the bullshit story about the rug and the insomnia?"

"He didn't ask what happened. The rug, the crime, any of it ... he never asked what the rug was used for."

"He didn't ask ..." he repeated.

She gave him her 'no-shit' look. "He didn't ask because he already knew."

ONCE THE DETECTIVES HAD TIME TO WALK AWAY, GIDEON leaned against the door, gasping, his heart pounding like he had just finished a run. He closed his eyes and pressed his face into the towel. "They don't have anything," he mumbled "Stay calm."

But they were way too close for comfort.

What to do? What to do? What to do ...

He had money stashed away for this. Leaving Pantheon would be a step back, but—

A sudden vision pierced his mind, one of a very dead Annie Cooper lying on the floor of the lab on Draco Station. Following that sight was a matching image of Libby Stanton on his bathroom floor.

He bent over, his hands supported on his thighs. "Libby was an accident," he moaned. He didn't realize she was

Senator Stanton's daughter until he returned from the river and found her purse. When he pulled out her driver's license and the name Stanton jumped out, he realized who she was.

"Oh, this definitely sucks," he said, shaking his head.

Libby Stanton's father was a primary supporter of Pantheon and Draco Station. Unlike the well-known International Space Station, Draco was a lawless mash of corporate greed and corrupt government oversight, where lab rats like Dr. Lazar were paid to experiment with human DNA.

When the government heard about the Draco Dragons created to work on the surface of Draco Prime by Lazar's predecessor, Dr. Eric Garwood, they were all too willing to back Pantheon in its god-like aspirations.

He snorted with genuine disgust. What do you expect from a company whose interior motto was: Where Gods Gather ~ Redefining Humanity's Boundaries Through Science

He shuddered and peeked out the window. The cops were gone.

"What else do they have?" he whispered, hunching his shoulders. "DNA? Witnesses?" They had talked with the girl in the store, but nothing he said or did was illegal.

Obviously, they were fishing for something to connect me to Libby, otherwise they would have taken me in.

A cold chill broke across his neck. Libby's purse was locked in his safe, along with the Draco globe. He had to dispose of her purse. "Drop that sucker in the incinerator." Afraid to touch the contaminated globe, he had placed in a plastic bag and shoved it in his safe. "That, too."

What happens on Draco is supposed to stay on Draco, only he broke the rules. Because of him, Lazar's Nobility drug was on Earth, right in his safe next to the globe and Libby's purse.

And then there was Annie. As value goes on Draco, she was no loss. But the FBI woman would eventually discover his connection to Draco if she dug deep enough. While that didn't connect him to Libby, it did connect him to Annie.

Tears came to his eyes. He dashed them away, realizing his career at Pantheon was undoubtedly over. But his talents as a chemist would get him into a country without extradition.

"A fake ID. A passport from Canada. A ticket to the Caribbean." It was going to cost him.

"First Annie, then Libby. Now this FBI woman is going to be the same problem. Damn these women poking around where they don't belong."

Dreya's brain was in overdrive making Gideon solid for Libby's murder.

I'm going to find out who this guy is.

"We need his work history and financials," she said. Behind the wheel, Morgan remained quiet. She liked that about him, and she liked having him drive—it left her mind free to think on the case.

All she had to feed her suspicion was Smith's thin story and his weak alibi. But from suspicion, a network of evidence could arise. Who is this Gideon Smith? What does he do? Where does he work? What other women are in his life? What other secrets does he have?

Secrets. Some were private, some fatal, some criminal. Me. Gideon. Morgan. Stanton. We all have them.

They entered her office with renewed purpose. She got

to her desk and immediately requested a search warrant for Smith's financials. His work history would come from public data bases.

Morgan leaned against a cabinet while they waited.

She sat back. "Smith's story makes the timeline for another murderer highly unlikely. He ran out and dropped this rug off at a public place and the killer took it home and put her in it and made it to the river within a couple hours. I don't buy it. The problem is, I don't think a judge will go for a search warrant." There were more than enough 'is-it-possible' points in her conjecture to rattle Smith's constitutional rights.

Her computer beeped and began printing. She eagerly reached for the pages, saying, "Work history ..." But her excitement abruptly faded and her mouth dropped open. As she looked further down the page, her eyebrows edged up higher and higher. "What the hell?"

Every page was completely redacted. His only available information was what they had on his driver's license. "Even his passport is redacted." She passed the papers to Morgan. He pushed off from the cabinet and flipped through them. His eyes went wide and he slowly shook his head.

Her bad feeling about this case was blossoming. "Have you ever seen a file like that?"

"Yes."

His dark look gave her chills. "Yeah. Me, too. This is government cover-up at its finest. I bet the warrant for his financials gets shot down. Dammit. Who is this guy?" With little confidence in a positive outcome, she added, "The only way we get past this is through a ranking official ... like the senator."

Morgan frowned. "He's more likely to impede us, not help. Look, I'm going to take off and go talk with a friend."

She rose to go with him.

"No, I have to see this one by myself." He hurried out without another word.

"Well," she mused, watching him disappear around the corner. "I guess some relationships are complicated."

Sitting back, she ran through her options, her finger tapping on the desk as if it alone could generate the evidence she needed. Her gut told her Smith was Libby's killer. But with no provable motivation and little more than a weak alibi to run with, combined with Smith's redacted history, she was still sitting on zero.

Zero doesn't get a search warrant.

Zero doesn't put him behind bars.

Her finger stopped tapping. She squinted. "Zero means he's going to get away with Libby's murder." Smith had some kind of protection. To her knowledge, this level of redaction came only to the high and mighty, or the good and dirty.

Her finger began tapping again.

Smith's wasn't the only place she wanted to search. Stanton was also on her radar. But getting a search warrant for a sitting senator was even less a possibility than getting one for Smith, especially one based on an agent's gut feeling and a piece of undocumented and now compromised evidence as bizarre as a feather.

Her phone buzzed with a message to come see the ME. She signed out a car and drove across town to the Forensics lab. Upstairs, as she stepped from the elevator, the smell of formaldehyde and antiseptic assaulted her nose. Beneath those pungent odors ran the subtle note of decay. She shivered, hoping she never had to have an autopsy. She saw Bailey and thought of him opening her up on one of his tables.

"Agent Love?"

"Yes."

"No Detective Morgan with you today?" he asked.

"He had an errand to run," she answered. "What do you have?"

"I have some tissue samples I want you to look at." He led her through the sliding doors to a microscope in the empty autopsy room. He turned on the microscope light and adjusted the focus. "These samples are from Libby. You can see the discoloration anomaly in each sample. I have identified the cause of the discoloration."

She looked into the lens. "What tissue is this?"

"Skin."

There was a small black squiggle in each cell. Dr. Bailey removed the slide and inserted another. "This is kidney."

There was more of the same black squiggle.

"Lung, heart, muscle, all have this."

"What is it?" She peered into the microscope as he inserted fresh samples.

"It's carbon."

She grimaced, not hearing anything she expected. Her not-scientific-enough mind scrambled for answers. "What caused this carbon to be in Libby's cells like this?"

His answer was slow, as if he was unsure what to say. "I'm still doing tests on that. Also, there have been ... other anomalies. Some tests had to be run over again."

"What tests are those?"

"Uh, DNA." He looked away quickly.

"Why? What's wrong with the results you got from the first test?" He clearly was trying to say something without saying anything. "Doc?"

He stepped back and stuck his hands in his lab coat pockets. "I can't tell you anything conclusive. Just expect more anomalies concerning this case."

His reluctance to speak made her think of Smith's redacted records. "Well, when you figure out something, let me know."

Back in the car, she pondered the complexities of this case. The feather was not an unconnected freak anomaly, but a critical piece of evidence, only she didn't know how exactly. This latest news of carbon in Libby's cells was another mystery. In no way did it remove any of her certainty about Smith's position as Libby's murderer. But Pantheon was beginning to smell, and the senator was right in the middle.

"All roads lead to the senator." The day had been long and now darkness was settling. Not knowing where Morgan was, she thought this an opportune moment to slip away and go look through the senator's house, seeing as how he was out of town.

But first she had to go home, change, and get her tools.

After leaving Agent Love's office, Morgan killed time sitting in his car. Politicians and corporations were an ugly mix because they work together off the books. There was one resource open to him for questions concerning 'off the books'. He sent a text, Poker game @ 10:00 PM and waited fifteen minutes before leaving.

He drove a few blocks to 10th Street, just a stone's throw from the Spy Museum, and parked. Inside a popular diner, he sat at the counter and ordered a waffle, bacon and eggs scrambled. When his order arrived, he poured an excessive portion of syrup across his waffle.

Before he could take a bite, a man sat next to him. Without opening a menu, he ordered what Morgan had.

When his food arrived, he treated the waffle with excessive syrup just as Morgan did.

Morgan ignored the man, but pushed a piece of paper under the edge of the man's plate. The man coughed into his napkin, sipped his water and wiped his mouth. He motioned for the waitress and asked for his bill, paid cash, and left.

"Whew," Morgan whistled. The unstated risk of these clandestine meetings always left him feeling like he just sat with a rat. Undoubtedly, spooks did things a rat would never consider.

He finished his waffle, wiped his mouth, paid and left. He texted Agent Love. *Where are you?* When no answer came, he ran through what he thought her options were.

Pressure's on, clock's ticking, got one lead with no evidence. She needs evidence. She'll go looking for it.

There were only two places she could be, at Smith's, or the senator's, but he knew she had no search warrant for either. He had gotten the text from the ME and assumed she took the meeting with Bailey. Where would she go after leaving the ME?

To harass Smith? No, to approach him would risk setting him on the run. That left the senator, but she knew he—

"Is out of town." What better time, he thought, to poke around the Stanton home. "She wouldn't. She has this upstanding by-the-book reputation."

She's her own authority. A little too much like me.

He started the car and pulled out, heading for the Stanton home.

At her apartment, Dreya dressed in black pants and a black cotton pullover. After wolfing down a turkey sandwich, she slipped a flashlight into her belt and a slim case of tools. A jacket covered everything she needed, including her badge and her weapon.

Full dark had settled by the time she got to Kalorama. She pulled up into the circular drive and parked just off the front door where a security vehicle would normally be in plain view. She checked her watch and was getting ready to open the car and slip to the front door when Morgan stepped up and rapped on her passenger-side window.

"For crap's sake," she muttered. She flipped the lock and he got in. "What are you doing here?"

"I could ask you the same thing."

She changed the topic. "Where did you go—to see a friend?" She sniffed. "You smell like maple syrup."

"I ate a waffle. And I asked a very deep source for information on Pantheon."

Pulling back with surprise, she asked, "Pantheon. So, you have suspicions, too. Who did you ask? What did they say?"

"If I tell you who, I'd have to kill you."

"Pfft," she snorted. "Can you at least tell me what you learned?"

"Yes." He showed her a text on his phone. *Walk away.*

"What does that mean? Is it some code?"

"No code, just two words of advice."

She inhaled with indignation. "So ... what? You take the warning and just walk away?"

"Well, I don't believe I said that," he defended. "I just wanted to give you fair notice. Considering my source, this is a proceed-at-your-own-risk warning."

"How extensive is the risk? Are we talking an official

reprimand? Demotion? Suspension?" None of her suggestions garnered a reaction. "Murdered and dumped in the river?"

"That's my guess."

His answer was matter of fact. His nonchalant tone made the words all the more chilling. She thought of the feather. She knew she was going to have to reveal the evidence to him soon. But first, she wanted something to go with it, some corroboration. Something from the senator's office. She reached for her door handle. "Stay here."

"What in hell do you think you're doing?"

"Look, if your ethical boundaries feel threatened and your compunctions are aroused, this is what you do. Stay here. Put your head back. All you remember is I got out to go pee; you fell asleep. I came back. You saw nothing."

"Great story. How do you intend to get in?"

"I have a lock pick gun."

"What about the security code?"

She gave him a slanted glance. He was getting indignant, waving his rules in her face. "I have the code."

"You have the code?" he challenged.

"I have the code." Her answer bounced off his incredulous face.

"You have the code or you think you have the code?"

"I think I have the code," she answered flatly.

His face was turning darker with each round of question and answer. "This dialogue is not productive, you know."

"It is if you now understand how it feels to be on the other end."

He balked momentarily, but continued. "Do you have the code, or do you think you have it? Because if that alarm goes off, I'm not sitting out here pretending to be asleep."

"The alarm won't go off. I have the code."

"What is it?" he persisted.

She exhaled hotly. "Get off me or leave."

"I'm trying to keep you from making a mistake and dragging me down with you."

"Leave or stay, I don't care." She waved off his concerns. "If this goes south, which it won't, you can just retire again."

"You looked at my file."

This was a statement, not a question. "And you didn't look at mine?" she rebutted, hopefully goading him into feeling bad. He clammed up at that. "Stay here. I'm going in."

"What's the code?" he asked again.

"The most important day in Stanton's life—the day he was first elected to the Senate."

7

DREYA GOT OUT OF THE VEHICLE, DRAWING ON HER GLOVES and leaving Morgan in the car. The circular drive wrapped around a landscaped center piece, shielding the entryway from the street. She approached the front door, put the small flashlight in her mouth, drew out the little torque wrench and inserted it in the lock. Next the pick gun went in and she snapped the trigger several times.

Click click click.

The pins in the lock moved and she adjusted the wrench. The lock turned. She opened the door and stepped immediately to the alarm keypad and quickly tapped in the numbers. She held her breath, betting her life on her profiling talents.

The keypad blinked green. She exhaled a gasp of relief.

"So, you weren't entirely sure about the code, were you?"

She jumped, feeling like she just rocketed right out of her skin. "Dammit, Morgan." She placed one hand on the wall while her heart banged painfully against her breastbone. "I thought you were staying in the car."

"I thought you might need some help." He looked loftily

down his nose, but in the end, he smiled. "Come on. Let's see what's here. There's got to be something, the political stench in here is suffocating." He waved his gloved hands.

She led him down the hall and up the stairs to the same office they were in yesterday; she pulled out her tools. He held the flashlight while she operated the gun and the wrench.

Click click click. The lock turned. She eased the door open and went straight for the senator's desk. Morgan drifted to the wall, scanning the framed pictures she examined yesterday when he interviewed Stanton. "Taylor is in half of these photos."

She sat and played her flashlight over the desk. "Hard to miss. He and Stanton are joined at the wallet is my theory."

Morgan strolled down the wall. "There's a public face of Pantheon, all PR poetry, and apparently, there's another face which we're advised against coming up against."

"Huh," she snorted as she bent over, pulling open drawers. "I smell an off-the-books, illegal by US law, unethical by western standards, black op entirely embraced by everybody making money off it. I want to know what's behind this." She sat up, shaking her head. "What on earth could it be?"

"Are you really sure you want to know?" He stepped up to a standing file cabinet. He removed a ring from his pocket with a collection of small keys and selected one, fit it in the lock and opened the first drawer.

His question 'did she really want to know' wasn't purely rhetorical. While a committed part of her wanted to solve this case, the voice belonging to that bad feeling she had from the beginning was begging to differ. She glanced at Morgan, he was deep into the file cabinet. Good. His compunctions aside, he wasn't a bad partner.

One of the desk drawers was locked and she used a pair of hand picks to leverage the lock and open the drawer. Methodically, she went through the desk, each drawer, locked or not, and each file. While some of it was unsavory, she was not surprised to find no evidence of anything illegal. Putting sensitive material here would be too risky, but the desk had to be ruled out. Morgan was working his way through the second file cabinet, leaving her to examine the book cases.

The wall unit was a massive complex of shelving displaying decor, mementos, and books. From ten feet back, the entire wall was a work of symmetry. Each shelf was compatible with the next shelf, with properly placed books, photos, memorabilia, awards and commendations. It was designed to be photo perfect.

And yet, something wasn't quite as she remembered.

With one elbow resting on her other hand, she put her fingers under her chin, looking for the fleeting change that had caught her eye. Morgan came to stand beside her. He mimicked her stance, elbow propped, fingers under the chin. She glanced at him. "At first, I thought you went out of your way to deliberately irritate me. But now I realize you come by it naturally."

"I'm wounded, really. Imitation is the sincerest form of flattery, is it not? What are we looking for?"

"The senator is a man of secrets. To keep his many fabrications straight, he requires everything else in his life to be … simple. Symmetrical. Balanced. Accessible. Always at his fingertips. And above all else, easy for him to remember. Hence the same code on the alarm after all these years. But something here is off. I remember this wall differently; he's changed something. I'm trying to figure out what."

He went to the wall, and ran his hand along the shelves. "Something hidden, perhaps?"

She joined him in closer examination, pressing at joints in the shelves. He moved to the center and pointed with his flashlight. "There, beside the vase." She pressed at random until she heard a click, and a two-foot section of shelf popped out on a hinge. She grinned and pulled the shelf open, her elation dying as she spotted a wall safe. "Damn. That's new."

"An alphanumeric keypad," Morgan said. "Not exactly a simple combination lock." He played his flashlight over the safe. "So, while the code to this could be anything, letters and or numbers, according to your assessment of Stanton's life, the code to the safe is related to what's inside. What do we think he wants to hide most of all?"

"He has his fingers in a lot of pies." She shrugged one shoulder.

"What pie gives him the biggest payout? What pie has the most to hide?"

"What pie," she asked, "is pictured most on the wall? Taylor. Phillip Taylor and—"

"Pantheon."

Dreya typed in PANTHEON. The keypad beeped and flashed a green light. She turned the knob and the safe door opened.

It was a deep safe with two shelves; both were filled with folders and papers. She pulled out the first folder from the top shelf and passed it to Morgan, taking the second folder for herself. They sat side by side on the floor with their backs against the wall.

"I got financials, bank wires, and numbers," she said. "Deposits, as in the seven, eight and nine digit kind of deposits. Yes, you heard me, nine digits."

"This file is contracts, proposals, projects—"

She got up and brought back two more files. "Here," she said, passing him one. As soon as she opened hers, the symbols for chemical compounds filled her pages. "No clue," she mumbled.

"All I have is lists of last names and first initial, with no indication of their purpose. Hundreds of names, by the way." He flipped through the pages. "Look. G. Smith. What do you want to bet?"

She collected the folders and was careful to put them back exactly as they were. On the bottom shelf of the safe was one large black accordion folder. She pulled it out and returned to the floor with Morgan.

They each took one of the two files in the folder. PANTHEON was on her file. She peeked at Morgan's file, it was labeled DRACO. She sat back, reading the top line on the first page.

Where Gods Gather ~ Redefining Humanity's Boundaries Through Science

She thought of the feather, and a sliver of dread rolled down her back, terminating at her tailbone.

Dear God, what have these people done?

She read on, squinting with revulsion the more she read.

"These are some nasty people," Morgan whispered. He frowned with a disturbing intensity, another indication beyond his words about what he was reading. Before setting the page down and taking up another, he looked cautiously around.

His action unnerved her. She checked her watch, and took up another page.

They read for an hour. Not another word was said before they carefully put the pages back exactly as they found them. Morgan rose and brushed his pants off while she replaced the folder in the safe and closed it. She reset the shelf and stood back to study the wall. Satisfied there was no sign of their activity, she turned to Morgan. He motioned, 'Let's get out of here.'

They retraced their steps and eased out the front door, silent as shadows. She started the car.

"I'll meet you at your place," he said and left to claim his car.

What she read in the files was so beyond her comprehension, she couldn't speak of it. When she got home, he was, of course, waiting for her. They walked through her door and she dropped the keys on the counter. She removed her jacket, the pick tools, and pulled off her gun belt and badge. She tossed off her boots, and padded to the liquor cabinet, returning to the couch where he sat looking very dejected. She had two glasses heavy with scotch. "Here."

He took the offering without a word. She sat next to him, sipping the strong liquor, hoping it would wipe from her mind some of the things she had read in the Pantheon file. The scotch didn't seem to be working.

Morgan gulped his drink like a shot. He got up and filled his glass, offering her the bottle, but she waved him off.

He sat. He drank. Still, there were no words. Halfway through his second glass, he finally said, "Now I understand."

She lifted her brows.

"Walk away."

"Ah." She waved her glass in agreement before finishing her scotch. She cleared her throat. "Ahem," she tested, uncertain if she could get her vocal chords to repeat any of what she read in Stanton's office. "Uh hum," she cleared again. Finally feeling capable of speech, she said, "Pantheon is altering human DNA to make hybrid creatures, and the government is funding this ... research."

When she rose to refill her glass, he handed her his, empty again. When she came back, he took the drink and wiped the corners of his mouth, as though preparing for something utterly disgusting to pass through his lips. "At a planet called Draco Prime, there is a space station and those hybrid creatures work on the surface of Draco. They're called Draco Dragons." He sipped his drink and looked at her, daring her to reveal something worse.

She knew the time had come to show him the feather. She wanted corroborative evidence to accompany the feather—now she had it. She opened the little box and pulled out the evidence bag. "At the crime scene, I removed this from Libby's body."

He drew back deeply and looked at her with you-did-what? She almost laughed at his pinched mouth, catching herself, and immediately turned his silent reprimand back on him. "Now that we know what we're dealing with, it's a good thing I did keep the feather. You know this evidence would have never made it into the file." She waved the bag. "It would have been redacted."

He gingerly took the bag, passing it in and out of the light. "It's pearlescent. How do you think it got on her?"

"It wasn't just on her, I had to pluck it from her body. She grew the damn thing." She waited for him to look back at her. "In case you're wondering, it's not possible. Humans don't have the DNA to grow feathers."

A deeply troubled look spread across his face as he absorbed the information. "The Draco Space Station is a top-secret installation owned by the government but contracted out to Pantheon."

He toasted her with his glass. "You were right. Very

secret, very black and definitely not on the books, very illegal, and I'm sure those deposit amounts were accurate."

She got up for the scotch bottle and brought it back with her; she splashed both their glasses.

"The money," he said, "comes from processing a mineral from Draco Prime, a very dangerous undertaking." He set his glass down and turned to her with the evidence bag in his hand. "So they create these creatures, these Draco Dragons. There are even second generation families who live on the station and work the mines."

He set the bag on the table. "How did something from an ultra-secret black operation lab get into Libby's body? For if she grew a feather, Draco Station is where the DNA came from."

"I saw the ME today," she said. "He showed me slides of various tissues from Libby's body. In every cell, there is a tiny black line of carbon. That's what gave her the discoloration."

"Did he offer any reason for what caused this?"

"No. But he's having to run some of his tests over, DNA tests, because I guess he didn't like the results from the first round. 'Expect more anomalies' was all he would say."

"Problems with the DNA testing," he echoed.

The statement connected the ME's words and Pantheon. "The Draco Dragons took control of the Station from Hammer Industries, the founding corporation. The Dragons had been running the self-sustainable station until Pantheon initiated contact. Only in the last couple years did Pantheon negotiate a contract with the Dragons allowing the mining operation to start generating profit again."

"When did Pantheon take over the station?" She remembered the financial statements. "The cash flow began in 2014, so—"

"Yep. Right about then. Stanton went to Draco Station on a private fact-finding mission."

"Of course," she said. "To find out if they can make money at it, that's the only fact that's important." She realized her assessment of Stanton finally matched Libby's.

"A fact-finding mission," he continued, "followed by several private meetings where Stanton greased some heavy hands in the back rooms of Congress, establishing government oversight with Pantheon in charge of Draco Station."

"Huh," she grunted. All this new information wasn't usable for purposes of prosecution, but at least she now knew what they were dealing with. Like Morgan said, these boys were really nasty. "But how did all this come to Libby?"

"G. Smith is the connection. Since we understand Pantheon and Draco Station, Smith's redacted passport makes sense. He must have been on Draco Station and brought something back."

"How do they get there—to Draco Station?"

Morgan's lip curled and he shook his head, producing a get-ready-for-it look. "That long list of names is, I believe, the people who are on, or have been to Draco Station. First, there's a week-long ride to a base on Mars—Aaron Monk provides the X Rocket. From there, it's a starship ride to Draco Prime."

Her eyebrows shot up. She couldn't stop her mouth from falling open. The level of corruption and deceit boggled even her jaded mind. "Sons of bitches."

She understood secrets when they were private; she had her own. But a secret of this magnitude screamed at her for exposure. She clamped her lips in a tight line, pondering the complexities of a government/corporate marriage. "Someone needs to break up this ring of silence and protection."

Morgan rolled his eyes at her. "Someone needs to watch their back if they're not going to walk away."

The scotch was finally working. She hated having a case evade her like this one did; the alcohol blurred the edges of her irritation. It also elevated her libido. Usually she would go out and snare a likely prospect for some horizontal action, but she didn't feel like going out.

Too bad you can't order a hot piece of ass.

"So, what do we do now? Where do we go?" she asked.

"It's late. I'm going home." He rose and went towards the door.

She stood. For a flash of a moment, she wanted him to stay, to kiss and hold her, and drive her to erotic oblivion. He was handsome and athletic. But having sex with him wasn't possible because she never saw her sexual partners more than once or twice. Going horizontal with Morgan would be a mistake.

Abruptly she bolted from her erotic thoughts. Morgan stood with one hand on the doorknob, watching her. Please, she prayed, tell me he did not see on my face what I was just thinking. "Maybe we'll come up with something tomorrow, you know. Sleep on it." She was babbling; she clamped her lips together.

He gave her a piercing gaze from under dark brows, pausing as if he, too, had a thought pull him from the moment. As quickly as she, he snapped back. "Yeah. See you tomorrow."

After he left, she reluctantly prepared for bed and settled in. Her head was filled with ugly visions of dead bodies, freaky labs on a space station, and humans that were not all human.

The senator; the feather; poor Libby.

And Gideon Smith, a man with no regard for the value

of life. She fell asleep wondering if the people on Draco and those in the labs and in the Senate were all animals. It was no surprise she dreamed of creatures that were animal one moment, human the next.

Gideon pulled into the parking lot of a dark bar in Anacostia Park, not far from where he dumped Libby into the river. His heart thundered with adrenaline and fear as he pondered the wild turn his life had taken since his last night on Draco.

"All I wanted was the good life," he whined. "Now I'm in this shit hole and having to run for my life." Suddenly his anger burst from his rigid jaws. "Damn you, Annie, you ruined my life. You deserved to die."

He exhaled and rubbed his face. "Come on, get it together." He was here at this miserable joint for his new identity, meeting a connection he made through his drug sales. The money, ten-thousand dollars for the new ID, five-thousand to rush the job, was bundled in twenties and fifties as he was instructed. He tucked the cash envelope in his jacket pocket and entered the bar.

It was dark. He stopped at the door to let his eyes adjust. The place was rank with the smell of spilled beer, stale cigarette smoke, and old vomit. His instructions said to go to the back and wait for a man wearing a cap that said Grandpa. Gideon sat at a table as instructed and ordered a beer. He pulled his phone out when he got a text message. He replied, *Here in the back.*

A man approached his table. Gideon was a healthy, conditioned man in his prime; the fellow wearing the Grandpa cap was twice his size easy, with biceps as big as

Gideon's thighs. He pushed the manila envelope of money towards the man. The envelope disappeared.

"You include photos inside?" The voice was deep and rumbling, the thick accent Russian.

Gideon nodded. "Rush, please."

"Always rush," the man answered. He looked at his watch. "Twenty-four hours. Watch for my text."

Gideon, his heart beating uncomfortably fast, watched the Russian walk out. As soon as he got his new identity, he could book a ticket. He held his hand out; it was shaking.

"Damn you, Annie. This is all your fault."

8

Dreya woke with the taste of scotch in her mouth. "Yuk." She moaned and rolled over. Her head was full of cotton, not a good state for an investigator. She walked into the shower and turned the water on full blast. As the hot water pounded into her scalp, she remembered wanting Rhys to stay last night.

Not a good thing having sex with a partner.

"But he's only my partner until the end of this case." She ducked her head into the water, rinsing suds from her hair. She put on conditioner. "All I have to do is wait it out. Then I can walk away when it's time."

Her lovers all came with a time limit.

She dressed and sipped on coffee as she tried to see the case with new eyes. Unless she could come up with something she was going into Smith's, whether she had a warrant or not. Her phone buzzed with a message from the ME. *Come by.* Another text from Morgan. *I'm here.*

She opened her door to find him on her doorstep. "Are you stalking me?"

"Is that what they call it? I thought I was giving you a ride to the ME's office."

"Your timing is good. I'm ready to go."

At the ME's office, they waited for Bailey to come get them. She stood with her hands behind her back, trying not to let her bad feeling about this case run away with her. When Bailey arrived, his expression was not encouraging.

"I can't hold these findings from you any longer. Come to my office."

They followed him, Morgan in the lead with her falling back, slowed by her increasing dread of what would come next out of this case. She caught up and sat with Morgan across from Bailey's desk.

"This is the DNA test results on Libby's hair from her brush at home; I used it for comparison." He passed them each a second page. "This is the test results on the DNA from Libby's body."

Dreya saw the problem immediately; a knot clenched in her stomach. "They don't match." She shot a look at Morgan. He kept his eyes down and held one finger across his mouth as if to prevent an outburst.

"How can that be?" she asked. She held her breath, afraid she knew the answer, yet needing to hear what Bailey had to say.

"As far as I know, it's not possible. But between the time she brushed her hair at home and when she was pulled from the river, her DNA changed. I was hoping you could tell me what's going on." He leaned forward, expecting an answer, looking from her to Morgan.

They couldn't tell him anything. 'Walk away' was their two words of advice. Once they shared what they knew, they were endangering not only themselves and their careers, but also whomever they spoke with.

Before Morgan could speak, she blurted, "Doc, you're the man with all the answers. Obviously, a substance Libby came in contact with is the cause. Have you made any progress identifying that substance?"

Bailey frowned, clearly unconvinced of her sincerity. "Preliminary tests on her blood indicate the presence of an ingredient ... not known on Earth." He dropped the incriminating detail like a snake in a punch bowl.

Dreya knew the ruse had to continue. She let her eyes bug with feigned shock. "What?"

Morgan instantly followed her lead. He shot forward to the edge of his chair. "Say again?"

Bailey grunted. "Really. That's your response? As I said, an ingredient not known on Earth. You figure that out, Detective, Agent, and I'll give you a cause of death."

She asked, "Do you know more about the carbon, the black lines in each cell?"

"Yes. In the cellular cytoskeleton, the b-keratin was reassigned, apparently due to the DNA change, into explosive growth patterns forming intermediate filaments, the type necessary for growing feathers, horn, claws and beaks.

"Something caused a change in her DNA, but her body was unable to handle the transition. After the process began, her brain shut down, causing her to seize. I could put Cellular Carbon Explosion on the death certificate for the COD if I wanted to lose my license as Medical Examiner. You have to find me another COD."

She licked her lips. Without cause of death, there would be no services for Libby before the senator's press conference. And Stanton was coming home tomorrow. She glanced at Morgan.

"We're on it," he said and stood.

She jumped up just as quickly, riding on his surge of

energy. "As soon as we get something," she added, "we'll call you." She and Morgan bolted out the door.

In the elevator, she glanced at Morgan; he drew a finger across his lips. She held her thoughts until they got in the car and were a block down the street. "Where are you going?"

"I don't know," he answered tersely. "But I had to get out of there." He shot her a dark look of warning. "You understand we can't tell anyone what we know."

"I know. 'Walk away'. What are we going to do?" Her phone buzzed. "Huh," she grunted. Her bad feeling was getting worse. "Go to my office; there's been a response to my Interpol alert."

"Here we go," he announced as he turned the car around.

At her office, there was a bulletin on her desk from Interpol. She read quickly, "Several deaths; authorities wishing to speak with the investigators on the Libby—"

"Love," came a shout from Assistant Director Jarvis' office.

She stepped in Jarvis' door. "Sir?"

He handed her a piece of paper. "You and Morgan pick this guy up at the airport. His name is Kingston, Quinn Kingston."

"Sir? About?"

"He's from Interpol. Wants to talk to you and Morgan."

There it was again—her bad feeling getting worse. She refrained from looking at Morgan and maintained a passive expression. "Interpol, here?"

"Just for you, Agent." He waved her off.

Morgan led the way back to the garage. Over the roof of the car she gave him a long look. "I know. You have a bad feeling. I do, too." His confirmation came with one lifted brow, not making her feel any better about this case.

They found Agent Kingston looking surprisingly fresh considering he just walked off the red-eye flight from London. He was mid-thirties, short hair, nice build, pretty eyes with a determined set. "I'm Special Agent Dreya Love, Agent Kingston. This is Metro PD Detective Rhys Morgan. Welcome to the District of Columbia."

Morgan and Quinn shook hands. "Agent Love, thank you for meeting me on such short notice. Please, call me Quinn."

"I certainly didn't expect a response in twenty-four hours from my alert."

"Alarming events have brought me here."

She looked around at the milling crowd of travelers. "Let's talk in the car." She glanced at Morgan, but he looked away, refusing, for the moment, to be a part of where she was going.

Kingston rode in the front; she sat in the back. "What brings you here, Quinn?"

"We just had a round of peculiar deaths across Europe."

"Deaths you feel are connected to Libby Stanton?" She shot a glance at Morgan in the rearview mirror.

"Deaths," he responded, "with the bodies displaying an astonishing level of anomalies; I don't know yet if they are connected to your case. Your alert indicated a skin color anomaly, but we are seeing that plus something entirely different. I'm here to find out if our deaths are linked to yours. Do you have a suspect in mind?"

Again, she looked at Morgan in the mirror. There was only one place to go; Gideon Smith. Morgan didn't say anything, but he was heading toward downtown and Smith's townhouse. "We have someone we like, but there is no substantial evidence. The situation is also ... compromised."

"Compromised? How?"

She hesitated. Once Pantheon was out of the bag, she was afraid the body count would go up. "The situation is compromised by the victim's father, Senator Stanton."

Morgan jumped in with, "Along with certain other power holders." His tone was somber. His quick glance to Quinn, chilling.

Quinn sat back, remaining silent. Morgan parked and pointed to Smith's front door. "We have a man with a redacted life who bought a rug, the rug Libby Stanton was rolled in before she was deposited in the river. This rug has an uncertain chain of possession, so we can't tie this suspect directly to her murder."

"You say he has a redacted life?" Quinn asked.

"The warrant for financials was shot down," Dreya answered. "His public face is a blank."

"His name?"

"Gideon Smith," she said.

"Doesn't ring any bells for me."

"We believe he is some kind of chemist."

"That would be right. Our deaths were first considered drug related, but the drug was like nothing we've seen. The bodies were frightening."

"What anomalies are we talking about here?" she probed.

"The first noticeable condition was their skin color. Our forensics have yet to figure out what causes this."

She checked Morgan. His lips were not about to reveal what the ME told them this morning. She followed his lead. With cautious hesitation, she worked into her next question. "Were there any other anomalies noted?"

Quinn pulled back and turned his gaze to Smith's door. "I'm only here to liaison between your agencies and European police departments. I don't even carry a gun. Officially, I'm as much diplomat as investigator."

"Unofficially?" she challenged.

"Unofficially, I want to know what would cause a human body to end like this." He pulled from his pocket photographs and passed them to her and Morgan.

Young bodies, all twisted and contorted in the same rictus of death as Libby. Their faces gazed beyond this world with dead eyes wondering what killed them. "What is that?" she asked, pointing to a dark spot on a victim's hand.

"A claw. Specifically, the claw of a cat."

"And this?" Morgan pointed to another photo.

"A tiny beak growing at the base of his nose."

She held a photo of a young girl with her head thrown back, blood trailing from her nose, foam on her mouth, eyes terrified with death. In between her breasts was a tiny spot of white. "And this?"

"A feather. Opalescent, and quite lovely if you like Frankenstein stories. As you can see, we are dealing with something ... abominable. I'm here to get answers."

She calculated the spread of risk as this case progressed. That the deaths were connected was apparent, but they had to decide if they were going forward. "Morgan?"

He took his time answering, staring at Smith's door. He spoke remotely, his tone flat. "We have information, not evidence, that a large corporation is likely the source for the chemical compound we think is involved."

Quinn inhaled sharply and huffed, giving Morgan a disgruntled look. "What was revealing in what you just said was how much you're not telling me."

"Ever have a case you wish you'd never seen?" she asked.

"Every single one. But this one—"

"Yeah, this one scares you, doesn't it?"

He swallowed, and she knew she touched a sore spot. "And well it should."

"So, what are you going to do with this Smith person?"

"I think the problem isn't Smith," Morgan offered, "but Pantheon, the corporation we suspect is at the root of this evil. Pantheon has a lot of government cover for what they do."

"Again, what I hear is how much you're not telling me," Quinn protested. He clammed up, nostrils flaring, his face turning red.

She held her hand out. "We are being evasive because—"

Morgan finished for her. "We think this case could be a killer. We've been warned to walk away. At this point I have to say you are well advised to heed the warning."

Quinn pulled his chin back, absorbing the serious nature of their tone. "You think this is a killer, do you?" He looked out the front window towards Smith's front door. "The photographs I showed you, some of those bodies were related to the highest in government, who have demanded answers. Their demands trickle onto my desk."

"Yep," Morgan, grunted. "That's standard, always the right hand against the left. What happens if you go home without answers?"

"I was told not to return until I had them."

Dreya cursed softly under her breath. "Well," she said, exhaling heavily. "I had hoped someone would be the voice of reason here."

Morgan looked over the seat at her. "I wouldn't expect that to be you." His comment lost its bite when he smiled.

"Comforting words indeed from a man who has a

revolving door relationship at work." She looked up and saw Smith's garage opening. His sedan pulled into the street and left. "Shall we?" She pulled out her lock pick gun and wrench.

Quinn took a moment to respond. "Breaking and entering. Can we go to jail for this?" He had his head tilted back, his slanted gaze filled with critical scrutiny.

"Let's pray," she said cheerfully, "that's the worst that happens to us. Ready?"

He nodded. Morgan pulled the keys from the ignition. "Let's go."

They walked to the front door. She crouched down; Morgan and Quinn gave her cover while she operated the pick. The lock clicked and she opened the door. They stepped in. "I noticed no alarm when we were here last time. Let's be quick."

"What are we looking for?"

"Anything chemical, anything that looks like drugs. Anything that looks out of place."

"So, anything," he said.

She moved into the kitchen. The modern space was pricey with top-end appliances and finishes. She opened drawers and cabinets, finding nothing of interest.

Morgan stepped into view and motioned her to come with him. She pulled Quinn from the spare bedroom, and they followed Morgan into the master bedroom closet. In the corner behind the closet door was a wall safe. "Get me a glass from the kitchen," Morgan said. "I have a trick I learned from a safe cracker."

She returned to the kitchen and reached for a glass when she heard a sound behind her.

GIDEON WAS TWO BLOCKS FROM HOME WHEN HE REMEMBERED the charged stun gun he left by his front door. Considering the dangerous company suddenly populating his life, he felt compelled to carry something for defense. He chose a stun gun, not wanting to be responsible for any more deaths ... if he could help it.

As he circled back around the block, he noticed the government issue car the cops were in when they came to see him was parked down the street from his home. The car was empty. He glanced around and didn't see them. "Dammit—I bet they're in my place."

What to do? What to do? What to do ...

He drove by, hunkered down and parked a block up the road. He raced back to his front door, his ears ringing with the roar of his heart hammering on adrenaline.

The door was unlocked. He eased it open, listening. Someone was in the kitchen. He picked up the stun gun by the door, flicked it on and stepped into the kitchen.

The woman FBI agent was reaching into a cabinet. He jammed the gun into the base of her spine and slapped his hand over her mouth as she fell. He caught her and eased her down, released the handcuffs from her belt and cuffed her hands behind her back. A kitchen towel filled her mouth.

He turned the switch on the stun gun again and crept down the hall. Suddenly, a man stepped out. He shoved the gun into the guy's neck and dropped him to the floor, twitching.

Gideon crept down the hall and into his bedroom. The detective was examining the safe. He rushed him and delivered the gun's charge to the base of the detective's skull. He went down in a spasm of pain.

Knowing he only had seconds before the other man

revived, Gideon grabbed the detective's handcuffs and darted into the hall. Returning to the detective, he used duct tape and wrapped up his hands and feet.

In the hallway, he wrapped the first man's feet and dragged him into the kitchen. Quickly, he wrapped the woman's feet with the tape. Sweat soaked his armpits and dripped from his face. His heart pounded painfully, screaming at him to run. But he had to stay and figure this out.

He ran back to the detective and dragged the big man into the kitchen with the other two. He stuffed towels in their mouths. Their guns and cell phones he collected and tossed into the toilet.

"Fuck, fuck, fuck," he muttered, pacing.

No way am I going down for this.

He went to the safe; all it held was the Nobility sample. Libby's purse and the Draco snow globe had gone down the incinerator at work this morning. He stashed the Nobility sample in his bag with all his cash. Once he got his new ID, he'd have to run for the border. He would slip into Mexico and then fly out to a Caribbean country on his way to South America.

"But what to do with these guys in the kitchen? If I leave them alive, they'll be after me. Fuck. If I kill them, I'll be on the hook for three more murders."

Fuck.

"In for two, what's three more?"

Fuck.

He paced. In spite of the circumstances and recent history, murder by hand was not in his skill set. "Dammit." He continued pacing. He looked at his watch. "Shit, I have to go meet the Russian."

The Nobility drug. Wouldn't that kill them? It killed

Libby. But why did she die? The Nobility sample was genuine, and was used on Draco without killing test subjects.

Like a bad dream haunting him, his last night on Draco Station continued to control his life. At that time, with Annie, as with Libby and now with these three, he faced a decision. Unfortunately, that first rushed decision on Draco could not be reversed. He could stay and face the repercussions of his actions, accidental or not.

Or I can run and hope to escape.

His lips set in a grim line as he decided. "It is what it is. There's no turning back." He put on gloves and pulled the Nobility sample from his bag. Using a toothpick, he extracted a minute amount and dropped it in a glass. Three drops of water and he mixed it up with his gloved finger.

His captives were recovering. Tears ran from their eyes and mucus pooled from their noses. The FBI agent moaned. The men were beginning to come around. At last, they regained a level of cognizance and stared at him. He squatted, holding the glass in his gloved hands.

"You don't understand—all of this was an accident. Libby touched something she shouldn't have and died. I never meant for that to happen to her. Hell, I was looking to get laid."

The three pairs of eyes glared at him without a trace of sympathy or understanding.

"If I remove your gags, you'll try to talk me down. You see, I can't take the rap for this. I never meant to hurt anyone. I just wanted to make a little money, live a good life, you know?"

He showed them the glass with the smudge of water and drug sample. "This is Dr. Lazar's Nobility formula, from Draco Station; it's how we make the dragons. No one dies on

Draco from this. I don't understand why Libby died. Perhaps she just got too high a dose." He shook his head sadly.

"Lazar hated the Draco Dragons. He was creating half-human shifter animals with none of the better traits of either humans or animals, all for corporate greed. What he wanted was to improve the human race.

"Animals were the higher evolution according to Lazar, not humanity. He was a fool, thinking he could create a nobler, more refined and disciplined creature using complex DNA activations. 'I'll make humanity more beautiful in mind and body,' Lazar claimed."

He shook his head. "Lazar was brilliant all right, I'll give him that." He scooted over to the woman. "Shall we see what higher form the beautiful FBI agent has within her DNA?" He pulled the towel from her mouth.

"It doesn't have to be like this, Gideon," she pleaded before clamping her lips tight.

"I'm sorry, but it does. Unfortunately for you, all of this is Annie's fault." He touched the tip of his gloved finger to the small spot of drug, and pinched her nose, causing her mouth to open; he ran the tip of his finger across her lower lip and replaced the towel in her mouth.

The detective and the second man were struggling in earnest. Gideon stood over the detective, who had slid down and was flat on the floor. He put his foot on the detective's throat. Not wanting to risk a finger getting bitten off, he wiped the drug into the base of his nostril.

The second man's eyes were huge above the towel in his mouth. "Wrong day to ride with these guys," Gideon commiserated. He dosed him in the nostril as he did the detective.

He stood and placed the glass in the sink and filled it with water before stripping off his gloves. "I'd love to stay, but I have an appointment and I really don't want to piss this guy off." He rifled the detective's pockets and removed his key ring. "I don't think you'll be needing these."

For a long moment, he watched them. They were still staring at him, showing no immediate effects of the drug, making him think again that Libby's death was an accidental overdose from the globe.

"Guys, it's been nice. I know how this is likely to go, and well, all I can say is, good luck." He calmly walked out the front door and locked them in.

9

When Smith touched his finger to her lip, Dreya closed her eyes. She scrunched them so tight, rainbow stars littered the inside of her eyelids. She remembered Libby's body and the evidence of her painful death, leaving behind its mark of fear and terror … and a beautiful feather.

No this can't be happening.

We got careless, one of us should have been left on lookout. Damn. Damn. Dammit. Now we're going to die. Horribly.

A flood of lost opportunities overwhelmed her heart and mind. Who would take over mentoring Kit; who would solve their murders? Where was the justice? Bitter and harsh, more regrets came.

I should have asked Rhys to stay last night. I shouldn't have let this guy kill me.

What did Smith say. 'This is how we make the dragons on Draco.' Are these my choices, to die or become a dragon? Is that an animal that's part human? Or a human that's part animal? A tear slid from the corner of one closed eye.

Someway, somehow, I will make him pay.

A tremor shook her hands and crawled up her arms. She opened her eyes. Rhys was flat on his back, his face turned towards her. Quinn had toppled over, all she could see was his feet and lower legs.

The tremor coursed through her body, up and down her limbs, rattling her heart painfully; she held her breath to facilitate the passing of the pain. Only it didn't pass. Instead, the pain shifted to a tingling sensation dancing through her bones.

The tingling became a sting. The sting intensified into heat. Heat sizzled, burning into every cell of her body. The squiggles of carbon in Libby's tissues came to mind as she succumbed to the fire. Twitching, she slid to the floor and writhed with her agony.

Her limbs began to contort, elbows contracting, feet arched, spine twisting. Spittle bubbled out of her mouth. As her eyes rolled back and her body started the grand mal spiral, she screamed into the towel.

Morgan thought if he could get his feet under him he could get up. But he slid down the cabinet and was flat on his back with his hands painfully bound behind him when Smith planted a foot on his throat. Before he could try anything, Smith swiped his nose with the deadly gloved finger.

The urge to thrash and fight was intense, but that would only speed the drug quicker. Stay calm. Think this through. He swore ...

We are not all going to die, not if I can help it.

Quinn got the same treatment as Morgan. Smith's words,

'Wrong day to ride with these guys' were a harsh truth. Morgan promised …

Smith, you're going to regret this.

A noise on his other side and he turned his head to see Agent Love. She leaned against the kitchen cabinet, eyes closed. A single tear slid down her face as a tremor worked its way across her body. She opened her eyes, and he saw pain, anger, and frustration.

His own painful tremor began, twitching up his arms and down his legs. His own anger and frustration flooded his brain. His own convulsion bent him backwards.

QUINN KINGSTON FELL OVER WHEN SMITH RUBBED THE GLOVE on his nose. He closed his eyes, refusing to give in to the primeval panic that was shooting down his brainstem. He knew to struggle was counter-productive, although at this point, death seemed imminent.

They said this case was a killer.

Photos of the dead were burned in his mind. They had suffered horribly. Why? Smith said they used this drug … where? And to do what? Make dragons?

From where he lay, he couldn't see either the agent or the detective. A shaking twitch snaked up one arm and down the other. Heat … deep, bone scorching heat poured through his body. The shaking grew into a limb twisting seizure.

Who will come to my funeral?

Dreya swam in a lake of fire, burning, scorching, shimmering heat. It drenched her, filled her, surrounded her, from the inside out and the outside in, along her nerves, within her cells, permeating her bones and exploding in her brain.

Fleeting images came of animals and humans, of swirling, opalescent DNA strands, and color too bright for her eyes to bear. She tried to move her arm over her face, but she couldn't. So, she tucked her chin and curled as best she could into a fetal position, the most primal response to pain. Unable to scream any more, she let the tears flood from her burning eyes.

I'm gonna end up on one of those autopsy tables.

Rhys was trapped in a sauna, wrapped, bound, unable to move ... to run. The heat was excruciating, razing his body cell by cell as he arched his back.

Crazy images danced in his delirious mind, images of flight, the sensation of wind lifting him to extreme heights. He watched the ground sink away as his mind ran wild in its death throes.

More pain coming now. He heard Dreya crying. If she can cry, so can I. Because his bones were coming apart, his organs moved about his body cavity, and his brain sizzled.

I will tear Smith limb from limb.

Quinn writhed. The agony took him apart, piece by piece, bone by bone, organ by organ. His mind ran from the pain by cavorting with visions both primal and visceral, bringing a calm comprehension to sear through his being.

I am the animal within.

Dreya groaned. She existed in a deep, timeless place structured only by instinct and the need to survive.

Survive!

The urge was beyond her control. Need and desire were reduced to simple frivolities, for the ultimate instinct was to survive. Air, give me air. She gasped, wanting to suck in a lungful like a man pulled from water. But the towel was obstructing her mouth, leaving only her flaring nostrils to fill the need.

She grunted, rolling to her side. Desperate to spit out the towel, she focused on controlling her panic over suffocating. Breathe slow, in, out, control it, breathe slow, in, out. Once the panic subsided, she opened one eye. There was no sign of Morgan or Quinn.

The panic surged. She closed her eye. Are they dead? Did Smith return with more rugs and a river destination for them? Where are they? She calmed her breathing and listened.

Not a sound. Smith was not here.

But where are Morgan and Quinn?

She scooted and wiggled, pushing herself into an upright position against the cabinet, gaining a new point of view. Still, neither Morgan nor Quinn were in sight. Her heart was hammering with dread, as it did when she walked up to Libby's tarp covered body.

Where are you, Morgan? What happened? She remembered, the pain, the burning. She did a quick check and noted her body was sore all over—from the convulsions? Tears filled her eyes.

Am I now a dragon?

A flash of something metallic and shiny caught her eye. She squinted ... Morgan's handcuff key on the floor?

This brought relief and panic again. He kept that in his pants pocket. Where is he? She slid down and wiggled over to the key, backed up to it and fumbled around until she had it in her hand.

She had done this many times at Quantico. She and her classmates timed themselves getting out of cuffs in various situations—tied to a chair, hanging by the arms, blindfolded and in the dark. The key was familiar in her hands and muscle memory took over. She closed her eyes and let her body remember how to unlock the cuffs.

The lock clicked and she slid the cuffs off. Immediately she yanked the towel from her mouth. "Huuhhh," she sucked in the air again and again before spiting and clearing her mouth. The duct tape came off her ankles. On shaky legs, she stood and ran water in the sink, splashing her face and wiping away the tears and dredges of froth, spittle and strings of mucus.

"My God, what did he do to us? Morgan? Quinn?"

By hanging onto the wall, she made her way from the kitchen. She came to a pile of Morgan's clothes and a kitchen towel and stumbled over them. She shook her head having no concept of why or how his clothes would be in a pile on the floor. She peeked around the corner and down the hall. Morgan was collapsed in a heap on the floor. A very naked heap.

"Morgan." Her voice was raspy and low. She sank down and touched him, afraid he was dead. But he was warm and breathing with a steady pulse. A flash of relief washed over her, but then she saw—

"No, please, no," she begged as she reached for a small black feather next him. She picked it up; it was beautiful, a deep glossy black with blue and violet highlights. "Morgan." She gently shook him.

Morgan remembered the pain of being pulled apart from the inside. His body ached as if he'd taken a bad beating.

"Morgan."

He didn't realize his eyes were closed, and actually wondered if he was dead. But he could hear Agent Love's voice, so he wasn't dead. Unless they were both dead and chatting at the pearly gates.

"Morgan," she said again, shaking him.

He opened his eyes, blinking against the dim light.

Smith's apartment; no pearly gates.

"What the hell happened," he groaned, struggling to sit up. Suddenly he realized he was naked. "Love, did you screw me while I was out?"

She gave him a disapproving look. "Confucius say man unconscious have no dick."

A bolt of laughter stalled in his throat at her incongruous words. "Dreya ..." Suddenly, a larger concern than his nakedness became apparent. The reason for his concern was her eyes. "Your eyes!"

She brought a hand up to cover her line of sight. "Come on, Morgan, you're horny and a prude? I promise not to look. Let me get your clothes. Where's Quinn? And how did your clothes come off?" She rose and worked her way back to his garments and dropped them over his nakedness. "Going to look for Quinn. Get dressed."

Quinn felt the cool air on his bare skin and didn't remember going home and disrobing. He frowned, noticing how sore he was.

Did I fall?

He raised up on one elbow, eyes still closed, trying to remember where he was.

What happened?

He opened his eyes and blinked rapidly, struggling to focus. Being on the floor in a bedroom he didn't recognize completely disoriented him. Suddenly, he remembered one thing. America. He looked down and was shocked, not remembering how he became fully naked. Voices caught his attention and he sat up.

"Ah, the FBI woman, and the detective." That much was familiar. What did they do to him? Why was he naked?

Agent Love appeared in the doorway carrying his clothes. "There you are," she said.

"What did you do?" he asked, glancing at his nudity.

She snorted. "You guys, it must be a universal dream. Get dressed. And no, I did not take carnal knowledge of you while you were unconscious." She started to walk off when she stopped and looked back at him. He instinctively covered himself. But she wasn't looking at him, she was staring past him. "Oh, no," she whispered.

Seeing her face clearly, he realized …

She doesn't know.

He wanted to utter the same shocked words to her.

Oh, no.

He knew what the words meant about her.

What do they mean about me?

Even more than her unsettling tone, her words were a chilling pronouncement. He wasn't sure he wanted to know what she saw.

She bent over and picked up something from the floor beside him. He barely got a glimpse of it, but the photographs of abnormalities rushed through his mind with certainty. Not really wanting to know, yet perversely unable to stop himself, he asked, "What is it?" What he glimpsed in her hand was ... fur.

He wanted to run—until she spoke.

"It's beautiful," she whispered. When she looked at him, she was not horrified, but instead, deeply moved. "So beautiful." She turned on her heel. "Get dressed so we can talk."

Quinn assessed his body. Other than the all-over ache, he noticed no other changes. He sat up and clambered to stand, grabbing the dresser for support. He limped to the bed, sat and began putting on his clothes.

He couldn't forget her eyes.

She found their phones and guns in the toilet. "Dammit, she muttered. Not having waterproof cases, the phones were dead. She pulled hand towels from a cabinet and wiped down the guns before going back to the kitchen.

Morgan and Quinn were dressed and sitting at the island counter. She handed Quinn his phone, and Morgan his phone and gun. They looked at her with big curious faces, then at each other. "What?"

"You haven't seen your eyes, have you?"

"No. What's wrong with my eyes?" She put her hands to

her face. "They don't feel funny. I can see just fine." She squinted, looking about. "Now that you mention it, my vision seems quite ... sharp."

Morgan took her by the arm. "Come. You need to see this." He pulled her into the bathroom; Quinn filed in behind and flipped on the light.

"Oh!" she exclaimed. She hysterically patted down her face, but all was as it should be. Except her eyes ...

Morgan whispered. "You were beautiful—"

"Now you're stunning," Quinn finished.

Her formerly sage green eyes were now a deep amber, almost whiskey color that seemed lit from deep inside. The shade was striking against her coloring, the effervescent light ethereal and ... mesmerizing.

"Oh, my God, what has happened to us." She whirled on the two men. "What about you? What happened to you? What changes do you see in your bodies? Your eyes aren't changed."

They moved into the hallway. She wanted to stay in front of the mirror so she could stare at her new appearance, but the answer to her questions about Morgan and Quinn was in her pocket. She drew out the feather and the tuft of fur, passing the feather to Morgan, the fur to Quinn. "Your eyes may not have changed color, but something sure as hell did."

Morgan took the feather from her, his insides quaking with fear and a creeping sense of revulsion. There had been visions of flying, visions he discounted as a standard human dream.

But he knew the electrifying and visceral visions he experienced were more than neural projections in his chaotic drugged mind. He envisioned flying because he knew how ... instinctively. His memory of flying was like a well-honed muscle, impossible to forget. He knew the wind in his face, knew his sharp sight could detect the smallest movement on the ground, knew the incredible strength of his wings—

My wings?

He rubbed his face, not daring to look at either Love or Quinn.

How is it ... I know how to fly?

Quinn was both enamored and repulsed by the tuft of fur Agent Love gave him. The fur was a mix of exceptionally soft black and silver hairs that literally sparkled with reflected light. Somewhere inside his mind and within his body, he deeply comprehended that the fur had come from his new body. A body that was more than he ever thought possible.

In his dreams, he ran with a pack; he remembered hunting and taking down his prey—

Prey?

"What do you remember?" she asked.

Morgan ran a hand over his face. Dreya's question was simple; his answer was not. "I was flying very high up, and I saw the smallest movement on the ground. It was ... euphoric."

Quinn placed the tuft of fur on the counter. "I was ... hunting ... taking down prey."

She picked up the fur. "This is not from a regular ... dog. I'm guessing a large canine, wolf?" She looked to him for help.

He shrugged, equally mystified.

"And, Morgan, a bird?" She twirled the feather, watching the colors cascade from black to purple. "Again, not from a regular ... bird."

Oddly feeling their pain and confusion, she looked from one to the other, frowning. She suddenly felt so connected to them, a wave of empathy swelled from her heart. She grabbed each one's hand, tears filling her new eyes, eyes that came with more than a different color—

Emotion. Dear heaven, their feelings are in my head.

She gasped, choking. "I won't leave you. I understand so much." She sobbed and clung to them with a fierce grip, oddly, not feeling like a fool. "We are different now; we belong together."

Tears saturated her vision, but she could feel instant relief coming from them at her words. Morgan was deeply relieved, but Quinn was still in shock. She released their hands and backed up, needing space in her head for her own emotions. She ran down the hall to the master bedroom and bath.

The entire wall above the bathroom counter was mirror. She pressed close to the mirror, examining her eyes. What appeared as light coming from within her eyes was actually micro-fine streaks of silver in her irises. She blinked, noting how her pupils quickly reacted to light. Curious, she leaned over and flipped off the light switch.

Her vision was incredible in the dark. She had noticed

the keenness of her sight in the light, but even in the dark, she could see everything clearly.

Suddenly, she knew Quinn and Morgan were talking.

They're worried; talking about me ... how do I know that?

She turned on the lights. Her eyes were stunning. "How do I hide them? Green contact lenses?" She put the lid down on the toilet and sat. Her mind was a clog of her own emotions and the whisperings she felt drifting in from Morgan and Quinn.

Am I telepathic now?

She rubbed her face. "Oh, boy." Looking around to test her new eyes, a spot of color in the trash can caught her attention. Recognizing Libby's phone, but afraid to touch it, she fished it out using toilet paper. "So, you were here, as we thought. Now, how do we prove it?"

Sensing an intense urgency coming from Morgan and Quinn, she hurried down the hall.

10

"What is it?" Dreya said rushing into Smith's kitchen. The urgent need in her mind was overwhelming. Morgan and Quinn were still at the counter. "We've been talking," Morgan said.

"About?" The urgent press was fading. She shook her head, wondering how to manage this invasive aspect of Lazar's Nobility drug.

"We remember," Quinn said.

"Oh." She exhaled in a huff. Apparently, she wasn't psychic or telepathic after all. "What do you remember?"

Morgan's voice was low. "We remember what happened ... to us. The Nobility drug, what it did."

"And? Are you going to tell me or not?"

"No," Morgan said standing up. "You need to see to believe."

He walked to the other side of the island and started taking off his clothes. When he was naked and visible from the waist up, he said, "Understand, I've never done this before ... deliberately." He closed his eyes and brought his fingertips to his temples.

She waited, holding her breath with fear and excitement. A hum abruptly fired up in her head; at the same moment, a field of energy emerged from Morgan and moved through him like a laser beam. He dropped from her sight.

Morgan!

I'm here.

She didn't speak the words, and yet she heard his thought in her mind, and he heard hers. The shock of this discovery paled when a large raven jumped up on the kitchen island.

See. I'm a bird.

I see you're a bird. And I hear you in my head. You're in my head?

No, you're in mine.

She ignored his comments, momentarily stunned by his surreal beauty. "Oh, you're beautiful." He was the deepest black, and yet he reflected blue and violet. "Do you understand me when I speak?" She shot a glance at Quinn. He was looking back and forth between her and Morgan as if he was following their telepathic conversation.

Yes. I understand your words. I hear your thoughts.

Quinn tapped her hand. *I hear both of you.*

Her eyes bugged and she plastered one palm to her forehead. She felt their emotions and shared thoughts with them. What part of my life, she cursed, prepared me for this? She exhaled deeply and looked at Quinn. "Do you have something ... we need to see?"

"Yes," he said, standing slowly. He walked to the other side of the island and took his clothes off, folded and placed them on the counter. Morgan twisted his head and squawked, purely bird in voice. She heard, *yeah, big boy, take it off*. She looked down, killing a grin that threatened to upend her barely held composure.

Quinn stoically chose to ignore Morgan. When he was nude, she studied what she could see of his body. He was nicely muscled, yet lean and rugged in form. His pretty eyes she noticed when they first met were watching her now.

"Ready?" he asked. She nodded.

He bowed his head. The energy field bloomed, and the hum in her head intensified. The energy raked downward over him from head to toe. Just like Morgan, he disappeared from sight.

"Quinn?" When no answer came, she looked at Morgan. He hopped to the edge, looked down and cawed. An animal rose, gradually revealing pointed ears and then the muzzle of a wolf. A shimmering black and silver wolf with ... Quinn's pretty eyes.

Her mouth opened in awe, amazed at the beauty created by Lazar's Nobility drug. Unbidden, she thought, *maybe Lazar was on to something.* "You both are stunning. May I?" She held her hand out to stroke Quinn's head.

Please.

She touched him. "Oh, you're so soft ..." He pushed against her hand, encouraging her to do more. She stroked him, luxuriating in the incredible feel of his exotic fur. The black and the silver played against each other in beautiful perfection.

Scratch please.

She grinned and applied her fingers to the back of his ears. A lite tap at her arm was Morgan pecking. He chirped. *Me, too.*

She touched the feathers on top of his head. "So, the transition happens just by thinking it? What does it feel like?"

Space travel.
Exhilaration.

"How do you transition back?"

Same way.

Just think it.

"How did you come to this ... awareness?"

Remembering the dreams.

Dreams when we were unconscious.

"I didn't have any dreams of being an animal," she said. "But I dreamed of animals."

You have another kind of awareness. Your eyes and—

Your sight, internal and external are enhanced ...?

"Why did I react different? Why didn't I become an animal?"

Perhaps you're the improved human—

Lazar meant to create.

She pinched the bridge of her nose. "Can you turn back. All this chatter is giving me a headache."

Quinn padded around the island. *Let me look around first.* He went down the hall.

From Morgan, *Go with him. I'll stay here. Inside not a comfortable bird place.*

She followed Quinn into the main bath. He sniffed the floor, running his nose over the entire surface, reminding her of drug dogs on the scent. He sat abruptly and looked up at her. *Libby died right here.*

He moved, sniffing again. *A tarp was here. Smith put her on the tarp.* He took off, sniffing the floor, tracking the scent back down the hall. She followed. He waited for her in the kitchen. *Hauled her out this door into the garage.*

"Well, now we know our suspicions were right. Do you have anything else to report before you ... transition back to human?"

Quinn yipped. Morgan squawked.

"Can I watch?"

Quinn barked and immediately shifted. The energy rolled through him like a wave. Before the wave, he was animal, behind the wave he was human. He shook his human body like a dog coming out of water.

"What's it like? What's the difference in how you feel as an animal compared to human?"

He began putting on his clothes. "There's a purity, an unbounded exhilaration of spirit." He shrugged one shoulder. "Hard to explain."

As he finished dressing, Morgan tapped the counter with his beak. "Ready?" she asked. He hopped off the counter to the floor. The transition was the same, a wave rolling through his body, leaving him standing on two strong human legs. As with Quinn, he shook himself heavily. "Whoa, that is so strange." He reached for his clothes and began dressing. "I have questions."

Quinn joined in. "Me, too. Like, what do we do next?"

"About the fact that you turn into beautiful animals that talk to me?"

"No, about Smith," Morgan said.

Quinn added. "I want his ass."

Her lips twitched to one side as she pondered the many unexpected questions rushing at her. "Priority, find Smith."

Both nodded.

"We want him, all of us," Quinn said. "Perhaps each for different reasons."

"Why did the Nobility drug kill Libby and the others in Europe?" she asked. "Why didn't it kill us, why did we survive?"

"What is Draco Station?" Quinn asked.

"Long story spelled Pantheon," she said.

"Then we need to talk to Mr. Smith, don't we?"

Morgan straightened his clothes, looking surprisingly

well considering what they had all been through. "He took my keys, but I have a spare set on the car."

"Where are we going?" Quinn asked.

"We could go to the office and put out an APB," she offered. "But I can't show my face until I get some contact lenses. These eyes are pretty hard to miss."

"I'd like to talk to Smith before he gets in the system," Quinn said.

"Me, too," Morgan added. "How do we find him?"

"I can smell him," Quinn said. "If I transition, I think I can follow his scent down the road, even if he was riding in a vehicle."

Dreya looked at Morgan. He lifted one brow. "Why not?"

"All right, then, do it and let's find this bastard before he gets himself killed."

Quinn pulled his clothes off and folded them again. He was naked for only a moment before drawing up the transition energy. He jumped out of the wave, landing on four feet. *Let's go.*

They exited Smith's place. Morgan walked towards the car while Quinn sat on the doorstep, sniffing. He lifted his head, testing the breeze. Soon he looked up. *Got him.* He bounded down the walk after Morgan, nose still high in the air.

Morgan pulled a key case from a bumper and unlocked the car. He opened the back door and rolled down the window. Quinn jumped in and stuck his head out the window. *I smell him, drive south.*

She took the front passenger seat. "Do you hear him?"

"Yep," Morgan said.

With his head out the window, directions were steady from Quinn. She glanced at Morgan and refrained from repeating them. The telepathy thing was both enlightening and a hindrance at the same time. Once they got Smith, she had a few questions for him.

Morgan finally pulled into the parking lot of a dive joint in Anacostia Park. "He's slumming. That means he's getting ready to run."

Quinn jumped out and stood at Dreya's side. *Let's go ask around, see what we can find out.*

"You're going in?"

He looked up at her. *I can be quite persuasive.*

"As a wolf?"

I promise not to draw blood.

The three of them darkened the door. Quinn slipped in first and waited. Morgan entered, she came in last. Her eyes immediately pierced the gloom, scanning every customer. She touched Quinn's head. *Can you smell Smith in here? Who did he talk to?*

His nose lifted and danced before he set a path for a large man in the back. She and Morgan followed.

The great wolf approached silently. The big man's voice carried his Russian accent. Quinn jumped up on the seat next to him just as Morgan stepped to his side; she stood in front with her gun exposed. The Russian saw only the wolf.

"Holly Christ," he shouted. He pushed back in his chair and reached into his jacket. Morgan grabbed his hand and relieved him of a gun. "You don't want to do that. We're only here to talk." He stuffed the gun in his rear waistband under his jacket. "But I'm keeping this so you don't get in trouble."

"Your name?" she asked.

"Lady, is big damn dog you got."

"Name?"

Predatory intent was clear in Quinn's pose as he drilled the man with his unwavering gaze.

"Vassily."

"Vassily, did you just recently do business with this man?" She slapped down Smith's DMV photo.

The Russian looked at the picture and shook his head. "No. Do not know this man." He tapped the photo for emphasis.

Quinn lifted the corner of one lip, baring a long canine tooth.

Vassily's eyes grew large. He pushed back trying to put space between him and the wolf, but his chair was already against the wall.

"In case you haven't noticed, Vassily, he doesn't like you," she stated. "He doesn't like you because he knows you're lying."

As proof to her words, Quinn's hackles rose, his ruff expanded.

"You should start talking, man," Morgan said. "He's had a rough day."

The Russian was pressed hard into his chair. "Okay. This man got an identity. Driver's license, passport. Rush job. He is Richards now. Robert Richards."

"Did he say where he was going?"

"No." Vassily shook his head emphatically. "Not a word."

The second canine came out, revealing the row of sharp incisors in between. Quinn shoved his nose into the Russian's arm, nudging him to look closer at the three inches of fang now exposed with waning control.

Vassily cringed and pulled his arm into his body. "All right, lady, call off the dog."

Dreya touched Quinn and he sat back. While his fangs were out of sight, his eyes never left the Russian.

"He said he had a bus to catch. That's all I know."

Dreya asked Quinn and Morgan, "Are we done here?"

Quinn jumped down and trotted towards the door with Morgan in tow. She followed.

Outside in the parking lot, Quinn put his nose to the ground and searched for Smith's scent. When he found it, he yipped and started for the street. "Wait," she shouted. "We go in the car."

She and Quinn got in the car when Morgan pulled up. "Go left," she said.

He already had the turn signal on. "I hear him, you know."

Quinn yipped and pulled his head in the window. He excitedly paced the back seat as they pulled into the bus depot at Union Station. When the door opened, he bounded out and ran to a parking area filled with busses. At an empty slot, he came to a stop. *He's gone.*

"We'll find him," she said, catching up with Quinn. "We've got his picture. We'll find out where he went. Come on. You're attracting attention." She put him in the car and went in the depot.

Morgan was speaking to a ticket agent. "We're looking for this man. We believe he bought a ticket here recently."

"Yeah, I remember him. He kept looking over his shoulder. What'd he do?"

"What ticket did he buy?" she pressed.

"He's headed south. Next stop is Fredericksburg, a little over two hours."

They rushed back to the car. Quinn had shifted and was pulling on his pants in the back seat. "Where are we going?"

"South," she said. "He has a minor head start—we should be able to catch up with him."

Morgan pulled out of the lot and drove towards the interstate.

"Thanks for bringing my clothes," Quinn said. "They came in handy."

"I thought they might. This business of shifting and leaving your clothes behind is a logistic nightmare. We're going to have to carry clothes in the trunk or ... hell, I don't know."

The drive south was quiet. Her mind was fraught with an endless array of questions; she was glad she didn't have their thoughts to contend with also. Morgan pulled into the Fredericksburg bus station and parked. "I'll go in. This won't take long."

While he was gone, she asked Quinn, "How are you doing with this?"

He snorted a bitter laugh. "I haven't had time to process. I don't know if I ever will, I mean, how do you live with this? What manner of life will we have, certainly not one you would call normal."

She was sympathetic, but she was having enough trouble keeping her own doubts in check. "Normal is highly overrated in my mind."

Morgan came back with a satisfied look on his face. "Smith asked about the closest motel, took a cab to a Best Western up the road."

They drove to the motel and parked; all three entered the office. She asked at the window, "Did this man rent a room?"

The clerk checked out the picture and then perused the three of them. Morgan flipped open his badge. "Official business. Is he here?"

"What did he do? Is he—"

"Is he here?"

"Yes, room 203. He paid for two days."

She pulled Morgan and Quinn aside. "It's 1:00 A.M. and

I'm exhausted and haven't eaten all day. What if we get a room and some food, keep an eye on his room and confront him in the morning?"

Quinn nodded. "I've been up for over forty-eight hours."

She asked the clerk, "Do you have a room with a view of this man's door?"

The little man looked over his computer screen. "The only room in view of his is 105. It has a single king bed, Wi-Fi." He looked them up and down, adding, "And we got the pay per view channels. You know the ones I mean."

"Just give us the room," she said. She passed him her credit card.

He ran the charge and she signed. He said, "Check out is 11:00 A.M. Say, those are some freaky contacts, lady."

She picked up the key. "Getting ready for Halloween."

They slipped quietly to their room, keeping an eye on Smith's door while staying out of sight. "Morgan, can you go get us food, and I need toiletries."

"On it," he said and ducked out the door.

"Quinn, I'll watch Smith. You look pretty beat."

"I am." He disappeared into the bathroom with his carry-on bag from the airplane, and soon clouds of steam poured out the door. She settled in at the window where she could see out, but had the blinds pulled so no one could see in.

She was worn out. The Nobility drug must have used all her reserves for she was running on the memory of fumes. If she was going to capture a fugitive, one that had gotten the drop on them once, she needed food and sleep.

Quinn came out of the bathroom, looking clean and near collapse. He wore a towel around his hips. "Nobility drug or not, I could be a new person after that shower."

His sense of humor was admirable considering what

he'd been through. His words reminded her of the Nobility drug. What was Lazar aiming for? What did Nobility seek to create? How do you select attitude and behavior from a DNA strand?

Morgan came through the door bearing bags from a drugstore and a Chinese take-out by the smell of it. "Oh, I'm starving," she said. "Fix me a plate and I'll eat from here. I can't take my eyes off Smith's door."

Morgan and Quinn dispersed food and they all settled in to make up for losing a day's eating. A companionable chatter rose between Morgan and Quinn as if they'd known each other more than a few hours. Waves of exhaustion melded with a soothing perception of security rolled off the two. Their sense of safety brought her great relief.

It's the pack. We're bonding.

She finished off her last spring roll and groaned. "Oh, who can stay awake after that."

Morgan drew an empty can of Red Bull from a bag and crushed it. "I'll take the first watch. You two get some sleep. I see Quinn's nearly dead."

"Thank you and good night," Quinn said. He went to one side of the bed, got under the covers and turned away from them.

"You sure?" she asked Morgan.

"Yes. Shut those pretty eyes. I'll wake you when I get droopy. I brought two more Red Bulls, just in case."

She crawled into the empty side of the bed. Her last view was of Morgan turning out the lights and settling in for a stake out. He adjusted the blinds for his view.

Her new eyes were so relieved to rest in darkness. She dreamed of Libby, always in need of attention, yet she pushed people away. Libby's face changed from the dead-eyed corpse to an amber-eyed blonde.

No, not me, she protested. Opalescent strands of DNA wrapped around her, surrounding her in a cocoon. Let me out, she cried. Let me out. But the strands held her; she was no longer free to leave when it was time.

"Hey." Morgan was shaking her shoulder. "It's still early, but you might want to wake up and shower."

"Right," she said when she really just wanted to ask, Why? The dream still held her; she had to break free—

Morgan shook her again. "Shower, go."

She took her bag of toiletries and staggered into the bathroom. She saw the time and realized she had slept over four hours; her body insisted only a few minutes had passed.

The water came down in a hot flood, blasting the sleep from her mind as she scrubbed down and washed her hair. She came out of the shower wrapped in two towels and fished out a toothbrush and paste. She reluctantly put her clothes back on, but was grateful for the refreshment of the shower. She brushed her wet hair and pulled it back.

When she came out of the bathroom, Quinn was up and dressed. Morgan crushed another can of Red Bull. "The light just came on in his room."

She checked her weapon. "Let's pay him a visit. Are we ready?" Quinn looked half-baked, but better than before he laid down. Morgan looked like a train cruising for a wreck. "Are you okay?"

His eyes were blood shot but he checked his weapon efficiently and with calm hands. "Fast metabolism. Must be a bird thing." He winked.

"He caught us unawares," she said. "Let's not allow that to happen again."

Quinn stood and began taking his clothes off, folding them as he disrobed. "He's not getting away again." The transition came rapidly. He shook his body, letting the final shimmy go down his back and off the end of his tail. *I got the hang of this.*

"I'll get the manager's key and meet you there," Morgan said. He opened the door and she went first, with Quinn in the middle. At Smith's door, Quinn sniffed the threshold. *He's in the shower.*

While they waited for Morgan, she pulled her gun. When he arrived, she nodded. He opened the door.

Quinn shot through first. She cleared the room with Morgan right behind. He eased the door shut.

Steam rolled from the bathroom. The shower turned off. Smith was humming as he exited the bathroom wearing a towel around his hips and another over his head as he dried his hair.

Quinn tackled him.

11

SMITH SHRIEKED.

Quinn knocked him to the floor and stood over him, snarling with all three inches of fang in Smith's face.

"Whoa," Smith cried, dragging the towel from his head down to cover his face.

Quinn, let him up.

Dreya holstered her weapon. The wolf looked at her. "Quinn, let him up."

Not giving in so easily, he growled and lunged for Smith's throat; he stopped with his teeth against the tender flesh, not quite drawing blood.

"No, stop, please," Smith whined.

Quinn backed up and sat, studying Smith intently.

In the respite, the naked Smith backpedaled across the floor to the wall, cowering. "Damn, what is it with you people. Why aren't you dead?"

Morgan stepped up and offered Smith a hand. "Exactly. Why is that?"

Smith hung on to the towel around his hips as Morgan pulled him to his feet. "What do you want?"

Dreya placed her hand on the butt of her holstered revolver. "We want answers."

Smith's chin jutted out in challenge. "I want clothes," he demanded. "Let me get dressed and I'll tell you anything. Hell, I figured you were coming after me." He made a move to enter the bathroom.

"I don't think so," she said. She picked up the only pair of pants and tossed them. "Hurry. Quinn's getting anxious."

A cautious Smith looked at the wolf. Quinn lifted one lip and rose on all fours. "All right, I'm getting dressed," Smith protested. He turned from them and dropped the towel, slipping into his pants without shorts before turning to face them. "What do you want to know?"

Morgan pointed towards the small table. "Sit." When Smith was settled, Morgan asked, "Why didn't we die?"

"You're not supposed to die. The Nobility formula worked perfectly on Draco."

"What did the drug do to us?" Dreya asked.

Smith seemed to notice her for the first time. "Your eyes … how's your vision?"

"Keen," she answered tersely.

"You're what Lazar was after. He called it human improvement through DNA enhancement. The Nobility formula activated latent animal DNA in the human genome, echoes from our evolutionary past. Ultimately, the theory was genius and worked so well, it was as though God came up with the idea. Lazar was relentless in his pursuit. The Nobility Project was his life's work." He asked Morgan, "What are you?"

"Raven."

"Yes. Lazar wanted to branch into avian DNA. And you?" he asked Dreya.

"I only have the eyes and the vision."

"What else?" Smith probed.

"A level of telepathy."

"Interesting," he mused.

"What else did the Nobility drug do to us?" Morgan asked.

Smith tapped a finger to his chin. "The Nobility drug worked for you, didn't kill you like it did Libby. On Draco, we tested for certain disqualifying genetic markers, but in hundreds of volunteers on Draco, only one was disqualified in this way. Libby must have had such a genetic weakness, a frailty that wouldn't support the transition."

"There were other deaths, in Europe," Morgan accused.

Smith pulled back, affronted. "What deaths?"

"Six. You killed six young people in Europe in one day."

"No, it wasn't me, it was Lazar's formula."

"Which should have stayed on Draco," Dreya growled. Her ire was on the rise; she leaned down to crowd Smith's personal space. "On Draco, your test subjects could get the genetic testing necessary before giving them the drug. You pedaled a get-high drug to innocent kids. Their deaths are on you."

"No, how did they die?"

"Like Libby. The same skin coloration from the carbon, and the bodies were found with animal residue, a feather, a beak, a claw. What happened to Libby also happened to them."

"Incompatibility due to genetic weakness, or overdose?" he mused. "I know I didn't put a Nobility overdose in the drug I made. I only have a small sample."

"So, death by genetic weakness," she accused, her voice getting louder. "That's your story? Seven young lives were ended, not to mention what you've done to us."

He rubbed his face, complaining. "Fuck. All this started with Annie."

"Who's Annie?" she asked.

"She was on Draco. She caught me stealing the Nobility sample. I had no choice but to kill her."

Quinn stepped towards Smith, snarling.

"As you can see," Morgan added drily, "not everyone is pleased with you and the Nobility drug. What else can we expect from Lazar's Nobility?"

Smith reached out to Quinn. "May I?" He looked up at Dreya. "Tell him I mean no harm."

"He understands you."

Quinn edged his nose towards Smith.

Smith placed his hands on either side of Quinn's head, gently stroking down his neck. "You are extraordinary," he murmured. "The texture of your fur is amazing, the coloring absolute perfection. You are better than nature could have created."

He glanced at Morgan. "And you're a raven. The complexities of human DNA. Hmm. Maybe Lazar was right after all." He gazed off for a long moment, lost in distant thoughts.

"What else?" Morgan insisted. "What other changes?"

Smith shot from his reverie, suddenly talking in an excited rush. "Lazar's goal was to activate the nature of animals, the natural point of view, if you will, as opposed to the human point of view."

"What's wrong with the human point of view?" she asked.

"You tell me. Your job is to deal with the actions and behavior created by the human point of view."

She shot a glance at Morgan; one eyebrow jacked up. Quinn added, *Point made. No pun.*

Smith continued. "The animal point of view is driven by instinct for survival. The human point of view is driven by hatred, greed, insecurity, insanity, sexual perversions, and a number of other unsavory engines.

"But with animals, their strict adherence to animal nature prevents them from the weaknesses we associate with human nature."

With elation, he looked from animal face to human face. "Don't you see? This is the crux of Lazar's research, what he was trying to accomplish with the Nobility drug. If the Nobility drug works on you as it was designed, you will continue to develop a nature that is more animal noble and less human despicable."

Quinn nudged her hand. "He wants to know why we didn't turn into dragons."

"The Nobility drug was meant to activate latent DNA. The Draco Dragons were needed for a specific job, so instead of activating their latent DNA, it was suppressed and specific DNA was inserted. The new DNA becomes the new latent DNA and bonds over the suppressed DNA. This new DNA creates the change to produce a Draco Dragon. Nobility is the base, but the DNA manipulation is a completely different process in making a Dragon."

She sat on the corner of the bed. "What else?" She was exhausted, the four-hour snooze was fading. "What other effects will we see?"

He shrugged. "I only worked with Dragons. But we noticed extended life spans and rapid healing."

"And the control for the change? Strictly at will?"

"Yes. The process was so on Draco."

"What about children?"

"As for the men, they can have children but they will pass no genetic alterations on to their offspring; the germ line is shielded. You, however, Agent, will pass your traits on to your children. Your eye color is a permanent alteration; an improvement Lazar would insist you be proud of."

"Huh," she snorted. "What do I tell the eye doctor who's going to order me the contacts so I look normal?"

"Yes, that could be a problem," he commiserated with a shrug. He looked down, suddenly frowning with lips compressed.

"What?" she demanded. "It's too late to hold any secrets."

"There is one more thing you should know." He darted a glance at the door, exhaled deeply, and finally said, "On Draco Station, there is little in the way of law. Actually, the corporate bottom line is the only law. Other than 'Thou shalt not negatively affect profit sharing', only one rule is cast in stone—that no shifters are allowed to return to earth. Once a Dragon is created, he stays on Draco."

His words were a death sentence.

"But we're not Dragons," Morgan protested.

A wave of anxiety and distress filled her mind. She put a hand on Quinn's head, stroking. He butted his nose against her hand, but she could feel his muscles bunched, his body stiff. *Easy.*

"True," Smith agreed. "You may have some wiggle room on that since you aren't Dragons ... and you didn't run from Draco. Everyone wants off Draco, so getting in is a lot easier than leaving. Look, can I go to the bathroom?"

Dreya saw his bag was on the bed; she checked the bathroom and saw no weapons or instruments of suicide. "Yeah, but leave the door open."

While he entered the bathroom, she looked at Morgan and Quinn. "What do we do?"

Take him in.

"I agree," Morgan said.

"What about us? What story do we tell? How do I explain my eyes?" She felt Quinn's misery. He was afraid of leaving them and dealing with his new condition alone. She told him, "Don't go. Stay here. I don't want you to leave us. We have to stay together."

Morgan agreed. "I think you should stay with us, Quinn. At least until we learn a little more."

Quinn pushed his nose under her hand. He thumped his tail on Morgan's foot.

"What's taking him so long? Gideon?" she called out. She stepped to the bathroom door and pushed it all the way open. "What are you doing?"

"I'm taking the drug," he declared. He had a glove on one hand. She could see the tip of his finger glistened as he raised it towards his mouth.

"What if you die?" she challenged. "What if you have a genetic weakness? How can you take the chance?"

"I'm a dead man anyway, Agent. I've broken my NDA with Pantheon by telling you all this."

"What does that mean?" she coaxed, hoping to talk him down.

"Breaking the NDA means I get shipped back to Draco to spend the rest of my life as a Dragon, if I'm lucky. So, keep your distance. I'm not going back to Draco. Maybe the Nobility drug will turn me into an enhanced human, a super hero, you know. The possibilities are endless—"

"Or fatal," Morgan said. "Put your hand down, Smith. You don't want to risk this."

"I'm not going to jail and I'm not going back to Draco." He stuck the gloved finger in his mouth.

"No!" she shouted. She lunged for him, trying to drag him to the sink so she could run water in his mouth. But he turned away from her and sucked on the gloved finger. "Too late," he said. "Too late."

Quinn crowded into the bathroom, standing between her and Morgan. Smith slid down the wall. He said, "I guess we're going to see what happens, huh?"

Morgan stepped out and picked up the phone. "This is Detective Morgan. Call 911, we have a drug overdose in Gideon Smith's room."

She knew from personal experience how ugly the effects of the Nobility drug were. Not wanting to witness Smith's suicide, or enhancement, however it went, she glanced away. Quinn turned around and left the bathroom, sitting outside but within view.

In the other room, Morgan hung up the phone.

She stayed with Smith, still unable to look. His feet scuffed against the floor and he choked. He made noises she couldn't bear so she put her hands over her ears.

Maybe he doesn't die. Maybe he becomes enhanced.

She lowered her hands from her ears to silence. She tilted her head, listening. Is he breathing?

Quinn walked in and stood between her and Smith.

He's dead.

She walked out with Quinn behind her. While she despised Smith, she had hoped he would survive the Nobility drug. Quinn sat at her side.

Morgan had the front door open waiting for the ambulance. "Take Quinn back to the room so he can get dressed. I'll stay with the body."

In their room, Quinn swiftly transitioned and dressed. "Holy shit, what's our story?"

"Let me do the talking."

They returned to Smith's room. The ambulance had

arrived and the attendants were looking at the body. She pulled Morgan aside. "What have you told them?"

"Drug overdose; and don't touch anything without gloves. I figured the less said the better."

"We followed him here," Quinn suggested. "Cornered, he committed suicide."

Morgan whispered, "We don't tell anyone about ... us. Dreya, get sunglasses and take a few days off, and take Quinn with you."

When Quinn attempted to protest, Morgan said, "File your report. Give them answers and they'll forget about you. That gives us time—"

"To?" She pinched the bridge of her nose, feeling a headache coming on.

"To sort some things out, don't you think?"

"I agree," Quinn nodded. "I would like a little time to think about ... what's happened."

"You two go," Morgan insisted. "I'll call this in and file the prelim. Here's my keys, take the car. I'll ride with the body."

"Are you sure?" she asked.

"Please, let me be in charge for a little while." A smile took all the sting from his words. "When I get finished here, I'll be whipped."

"Come to my place," she said. Why she blurted that, she couldn't guess. She had only one bed. But the tug to stay with these two was irresistible. "I can't explain it. But—"

Morgan put his hand on her shoulder. "I understand." He looked at Quinn and they nodded as though they shared thoughts. "We're connected now. I feel it. I don't know what this connection means, but I can't ignore the need for us to stay together." He rubbed his face. "What the hell."

"Finish up," she said with concern. "You've been up all night. Bird or not, you need rest."

"We'll be waiting," Quinn added.

She drove to her apartment. Once there, they entered and she tossed Morgan's keys on the side table next to her gun belt.

Quinn stood with his hands in his pockets. "I don't know what to do. I don't know where to go. I don't know where I belong."

She held her hand out. "I know you belong with us. Lazar's Nobility has made us family. Huh," she snorted. "Not what I thought I'd come home with today."

"Can we lay down? Don't get me wrong. I'm not making a play for sex, although you can give me a chance tomorrow." He winked one of his pretty eyes.

"Come on." She pulled him into the bedroom. They stripped down to their underwear and crawled beneath the covers. She lay on her back staring at the ceiling. Inside her head was a mash up of confusion, exhaustion, and anxiety.

I'm different. I don't know what I am.

Me, too.

She started. "I thought telepathy only happened when you were in animal form."

"I don't know the rules," he said. "But I feel your emotions, I hear your thoughts. Perhaps it has to do with the exhaustion ... or maybe the emotional distress?"

She rolled on her side and captured one of his hands. His pretty eyes were sad and clouded with confusion, matching her emotions. "Everything's going to be all right. You're going to be okay."

"How do you know?"

She half-heartedly rolled a shoulder. "I don't know the

future, but I know when you quit, you lose all autonomy, so I keep going."

"You like to be in control?"

"I like knowing what I can count on. Until today, what I counted on was me."

"And now us?"

Her gaze wandered past him, unsure of the words he needed to hear. Inside, she imagined the Nobility drug chipping away at her DNA, routing out the old human point of view, bringing in the nobler perspective of nature.

The change was there, subtle, and yet hard to miss. She always counted on her need to escape to prevent her from becoming emotionally entangled. But the old instinctive compulsion to run away was being overwhelmed by a new drive, a new instinct commanding her to connect and support.

Survival. The pack. Stronger together than apart.

"We belong together. That's all I know right now."

He closed his eyes and gripped her hands. A tear rolled free.

"Do you have family?" she asked. "A girlfriend ... at home in Europe?"

"No. The work—you know how it is. I've been alone for some time. Seemed better that way."

"Yeah," she exhaled with resignation. She pulled him into her arms, placing his head on her chest. "Alone always used to be the way."

"Not anymore?"

Oddly, his closeness calmed her distress, and in return she felt his lessen. Weak apart. Stronger together.

This is not how I have lived my life.

"Not anymore," she agreed. She stroked his head, remembering the feel of his fur under her fingertips. Just getting her mind to wrap around their animal aspects was going to take a while. The turmoil of telepathy combined with the uncertainty of Nobility to create a maelstrom in her thoughts. "Morgan was right. We need time to figure this out."

"I'll send in a report later today. Afterwards, I have some time coming I can use."

"Good." She kissed the top of his head, not from sexual desire, but from an outpouring of care and concern. The truth was, she desired both Quinn and Morgan. But not in her usual love-em-and-leave-em fashion.

We must mate to cement the pack.

This foreign thought made her eyes bug and her heart ramp up, not with aversion, but with excitement. Normally few men would go for this, but—

We're different. We're Nobility.

She pulled Quinn close, feeling the calm spread from her to him. His heart rate slowed and his breathing relaxed into longer, deeper breaths.

How this change was going to affect her life was a mystery. Where they might end up, she couldn't begin to speculate. It was a new world, one with different rules, a different mode of operations. She sighed, wondering ...

How do I bed them both?

There was no easy answer, much less one that was familiar. She closed her eyes and let her mind drift. Sleep came with images ... and emotion.

The freedom was exalting, exhilarating, and euphoric. She and Morgan and Quinn were no longer held by human expectations, human subjectivity, or human limitations. They were bound only by the need for survival of the pack. Apart they were weak.

Stronger. Together. Connected.

She floated among DNA strands. Opalescent, iridescent, sparkling, the strands pulsed with life. Before her, they came together and formed a circle that separated into pieces, the parts twirling and dancing together, unconnected, yet coordinated. She reached for the pieces in order to hold them. One came into her hand, and another. She placed them end to end and grabbed one more. They fit together, stronger.

But one piece danced just out of her reach ...

The dream was interrupted by her being gently pushed over towards Quinn. She vaguely felt a weight sinking onto the bed behind her. *Rhys?*

I'm here. Go back to sleep.

She relaxed and drifted again. Memory of the incomplete circle flitted through her mind, teasing her with possibility.

Hours later, the smell of coffee and the sound of male chatter broke into her rising consciousness. There was cold bed space in front and behind her, causing her to curl her legs up for warmth. She opened one eye briefly, long enough to see light still came through the windows. "It must be afternoon."

Quinn and Rhys' voices were recognizable, although she couldn't hear what they were saying. With her eyes closed, she thought of them, saw their faces in her mind. First came Quinn; he was relaxed. Bonding. Then Rhys' emotions eased into her mind. He was agreeable, companionable. Bonding.

That is noble.

She got out of bed and went to the bathroom. Her eyes were still a shock with their color and the ethereal look of light. "Lazar. What have you done to me?" Everything else seemed the same. She washed her face, brushed her teeth and put her hair up while she took a few minutes to shower.

Finally feeling alive again, she released her hair and tugged on old shorts and a tee shirt.

In the kitchen, Quinn and Rhys were chuckling. Rhys had a cup of coffee poured and pressed it into her hands. "Feel better?"

"Yes." She sipped the coffee. Black and hot. Perfect. "What are you two cooking up?" She peeked over the counter and saw Quinn had raided the refrigerator and was preparing breakfast. "Food first," he said. "Then answers."

He was a good cook and they feasted heartily. She couldn't remember being so hungry, and wondered if the increased appetite was an effect of Nobility. After polishing off eggs and potatoes, she wiped her plate clean with the last of her toast and sat back. Suddenly, she realized they were sharing breakfast ... and it felt good.

The moment was surrealistic. There was this presence of comradeship—no, more than that, it was the feeling of family. "Do you feel this attachment thing among us, or am I the only one?"

Quinn set his cup down. "I feel deeply connected to the both of you. I can't describe or explain adequately, but I ... I can't leave you."

"Whew," Rhys whistled. "I thought I was the only one. But Quinn and I have been talking, and I feel like he is a part of me ... as you are, Dreya."

She frowned. She just wanted to understand. She hated not understanding something. "Do you think this connection is because of these ... shared emotions ... the telepathy?"

"Because I genuinely care for you," Quinn offered, "and that is established, I am more aware of you. I—"

Rhys broke in. "This means my treatment of you is subject to those feelings and the higher Nobility awareness.

That, it seems, results in a more noble approach, would you say?"

"Yes," Quinn agreed.

"It makes sense. I guess." She rubbed her face in frustration. "I feel like I'm walking in the dark."

Her phone buzzed and she groaned. "It's starting already." She glanced at the clock and realized her idea of already was in reality much later in the afternoon than she thought. She saw the caller ID and whispered, "Jarvis." Rhys went to the bathroom and turned on the shower.

She answered, "Love. Yes, sir. Yes, sir. Yes, sir, right away, sir." She hung up, exhaling with relief. "Whew. Tell Rhys to hurry up. You're in there next." She put the phone down and went to change clothes. "Jarvis. He isn't happy."

12

Wearing her darkest sunglasses, Dreya walked into her office with Rhys and Quinn behind her. She made a quick pass by her desk looking for messages. The only one waiting for her was from Jarvis. "We have to take care of this." She kept her glasses on, and with her two partners in tow, proceeded to the Assistant Director's office.

"Sir." She stood in his doorway waiting for him to acknowledge her. When he looked up, she wished she stayed home. "Sir?"

"Do you plan on making a report sometime today? Perhaps when you get around to it," he snapped.

"I was indisposed earlier today."

He drilled her with a direct look and a painful frown. She could see him trying to look through her sunglasses. "And take those shades off. You're inside."

She licked her lips and put her hands behind her back, crossing her fingers. "Sir, I burned my eyes and have to keep the glasses on for ... a short while." She fixed her gaze over his shoulder, unable to give him a direct look. He craned his neck to look past her at Rhys and Quinn. Seeing them, his expression, in fact, did not soften, only deepened.

"And what do you two have to say?"

Rhys cleared his throat. "About what, sir? I made my report this morning. My Chief sent you a copy?"

"Oh, I have it all right." Jarvis pushed papers around on his desk, pulling out Morgan's report. "Let's see, ah, here it is." He looked up, lifting one eyebrow and cocking his head. "If I may paraphrase ... we arrived; suspect committed suicide by taking a drug; we called the EMS."

She looked down, not daring to grin. She knew how few words Morgan could use when he was in the mood.

Jarvis relinquished his dry humor. "Agent Love, I am waiting for your report. In this report, you'll explain how you managed to find Smith. I'd also like to know how the suspect obtained the drug after you had him in custody. I'd like to know ... everything that is not in Detective Morgan's report. Go to your desk and do not leave until I have your report in my hand. Do you understand?"

She took a small step backward and spun on her heel when Jarvis added, "I know a secret when I smell one, Love." Without a glance back, she answered, "Yes, sir."

Once in the safety of her office, she closed the door behind Quinn and Rhys. Quinn sat in her chair. Rhys leaned against the wall and stuffed his hands in his pockets. She paced. "How much do we tell?"

"Tell them we're no longer fully human?" Morgan asked.

"And technically illegal by Draco law?" Quinn added. He frowned. "Oh, did I forget to factor in the wiggle room we might claim concerning those technicalities."

His disparaging words were followed by a chuckle. But his pretty eyes were strained with despair, a despair that was flooding her mind. She put a hand on his shoulder. "You're not alone in this. No matter what we do, no matter what happens, we stick together."

She detected a rush of ease from him at her touch; her words soothed him further. Rhys' emotions were less chaotic than Quinn's, but she could feel his struggling sense of ineptitude over how to handle their quandary. Catching his eye, she said, "I don't know what to do, either."

"Just who do we tell?" he whispered. "If we tell Jarvis, can we trust him with ... our secret. The man's a little too astute for me. I don't relish you having to keep this from him."

"And what happens to us if you do?" Quinn asked. "I have no desire to end up a test subject in a lab ... on Draco Station."

"Can he protect us?" Rhys asked. He pushed off the wall. "Can he give us cover if we tell him?"

"I don't know," she moaned.

"If we don't tell anyone," Quinn asked, "how do we stay together?"

His question echoed her thoughts. Especially since she bore irrefutable and very visible evidence of something not normal. The questions likely to arise from an eye doctor worried her. She took a deep breath and blurted, "We walk away from our lives and go underground." There. She threw it out, just testing the waters.

"A fugitive for life?" Rhys said. "I can't live with that."

Quinn shook his head. "Me, either."

"So, we're down to two options. We try to hide it, or we tell. Which of those can you live with?"

Silence moved in. She had to shut her mind from their thoughts and feelings or be swamped. Her own rampant emotions begged to bound out of control. A strong part of her wanted to tell the world their secret ... to stand at a press conference and pull her sunglasses off.

But she was no longer making decisions for one.

Quinn stared off into nothingness. Rhys pondered his shoes. Uneasy with making all the decisions, she waited for them to speak.

"Jarvis. Is he a good man?" Quinn said softly.

"One of the best. He's been around a long time, has a lot of goodwill stored up," she said. "He's one of the few people, actually, now that I think about it, he's the only person I'd trust with this secret."

Quinn retreated into his lost gaze. She looked at Rhys; he went back to inspecting his shoes. "Don't leave me to make this decision alone," she protested. "You have to say something. Rhys?"

"Our number one priority is staying safe, which means staying together." He gave them each a direct look. She nodded eagerly.

Quinn followed, saying, "Yes, I know that ... on an instinctive level. We are essential to each other's survival."

"How do we find a way to stay together?" she asked. "What do we do, quit and become a private team? Selling ourselves to the highest bidder?"

"No," Rhys said. "We can't openly market our ... uniqueness."

"But I like the team idea," Quinn added. "I like that a lot."

She felt his acceptance wrap him in comfort. The idea of a team appealed to her as well. "Rhys?" He nodded. She could feel him warming up to the idea.

"With our uniqueness, we'd make a hell of a team. But it would still be under the radar. We're back to not telling anyone. At the very least," she lamented, "I'll be living behind sunglasses."

"What if we talk to Jarvis," Quinn suggested. "Share the situation with him, and see what he advises. He already smells a secret."

She agreed. "The man has a very strong sense of smell." Her phone buzzed and she looked at the message. "Huh. It's Jarvis. He wants to see us."

Rhys raised his eyebrows. Quinn shrugged.

They went back to Jarvis' office. They could see he was on the phone, a hand covering his free ear. He finished his conversation and motioned them in. Dreya saw the steel in his eye and took a seat before the desk, Rhys took the other chair. Quinn pulled a chair over and joined them.

Jarvis stared at them for a long moment ... long enough for her to want to squirm in her seat. She resisted, calming her heart rate. Finally, Jarvis' lips broke their rigid line and he cleared his throat several times.

Uh oh, she thought. Something ugly coming.

"Ahem," he mumbled and pulled on his ear.

Never had she seen her boss so flustered, much less at a loss for words. She held her breath and leaned forward, squinting at him behind her sunglasses.

"I have been on the phone," he announced.

Unable to hold still any longer, she shifted in her seat. This, she thought, is not good. She was reminded of the bad feeling that had followed her through this case.

They waited for the obviously difficult words to come. In her peripheral vision, she saw Rhys and Quinn also leaning forward. The room went still; the breath she held seemed to leave the office in a vacuum. She braced herself as Jarvis spoke.

"I have had several conversations ... with people so far

above my pay grade, I didn't know they existed ... until this case. I was ... allowed these conversations even though—"

He raised one hand as if to stop himself, then calmly placed the hand back in his lap. "I was graced with these conversations even though my security clearance was insufficient."

She licked her lips. Rhys sat up like a piece of rebar was rammed down his spine. Quinn scooted back in his seat so forcefully his chair tipped; he slammed his feet on the floor as the chair threatened to topple over.

Jarvis shot a look across them. When he spoke, his tone was frighteningly void of inflection. "I am not going to ask you any questions. Love. What I demanded of you earlier is rescinded; forget your report. I'll be filing your report."

He templed his fingers in front of his face and stared at them from under heavy brows. "Since I am not allowed to ask you any questions, all I can do is give you travel orders."

"Travel?" she asked. "Where are we going? What case?" She swallowed and resisted looking at Rhys and Quinn.

"Oh, it's the same case with a new victim," Jarvis said. "One Annie Cooper has been murdered. The powers that be —the ones I didn't know existed—they want you investigating her death along with another murder." He paused to rake his eyes across them.

"You're going to Draco Station."

THE END

The Dreya Love series is a total of 5 books that complete the main character arcs. Although finished, I set the ending up with the potential for more 'episodes' as the team moves on to work under special orders.

The series is currently being translated into Italian, German, Spanish, and Dutch.

ABOUT THE AUTHOR

Dana Lyons is a USAToday Best Selling Author and an International Best Seller. She was voted one of 50 Great Writers You Should Be Reading in 2015 and 2016. She is multi-published with full length novels and novellas in ebook, audio, and print.

Other works by Dana Lyons:

Blood and Fire Dreya Love Book 2 ~ On a black-ops space station, a blood thirsty dragon shifter goes on a killing spree—until Dreya and her team get in the way.

**Inhuman? Exceptional? Noble?
They seek their maker.**

Welcome to the backside of hell—Draco Station.

Draco Station is an ultra-secret installation over the planet Draco Prime where mining Vulkillium is a mega billion-dollar business. But to work the surface you need a special kind of human—a Draco Dragon.

When bodies start turning up on the space station, Dreya Love and her team set out to investigate, and come face to face with Dr. Anthony Lazar. Dr. Lazar is brilliant. Unfortunately for humanity, he's also insane. He has a vision of humanity's future and the tools to implement his twisted ideals. After all, he is smarter than God.

A madman, a dragon with dreams of blood and fire, and a sheriff with a grudge—all complicate the search for answers. If Dreya's not careful, she and her team could end up dead ... or worse.

Follow FBI Special Agent Dreya Love and her men, Rhys Morgan, and Quinn Kingston as their lives change and entwine ... forever ... in ways they could never imagine!

Secrets Dreya Love Book 3 ~ A serial killer is murdering for love, and he has Dreya Love in his sights.

There's no going back for a little boy denied love.

Martin Nash was once seven years old and longed for words of love from his mother. At thirty-five, he knows he's never going to hear them from her. But he's willing to kill for as long as it takes ... until someone tells him the words.

Nobility transformed them and their lives.

Nobility, a genetic modification created by Dr. Anthony Lazar, uses latent animal DNA to cage the human ego and bring mankind to a higher moral code free of envy, greed, and jealousy. Noble means possessing an exceptional character in the face of adversity.

As Dreya, Rhys, Quinn, and Simon discover the dangerous position they're in by being Noble, they search for a way to fit exceptional into their everyday life. While old habits provide a never-ending challenge going forward, there's no going back.

In the midst of this uncertainty, Dreya puts herself in the line of fire with a serial killer who has a fetish for eyeballs. What she doesn't know is ...
Nothing is safe and nowhere is private.

It's not a good time to have secrets.

Sole Survivor Dreya Love Book 4 ~ A haunted forest, a broken man, a pack fighting for survival.

Can Dreya and the boys heal Quinn's pain, or is staying a wolf the only answer for him?

Sasha Ivanov, sold as a young boy into slavery, becomes a monster in the relentless drive to never be a victim again. Deemed the worst of the worst by Dr. Anthony Lazar, the geneticist who wants to remake the human race, Sasha discovers he will never be the same.

Quinn Kingston knows what Dr. Lazar can do from personal experience. But as a Nobilized and highly evolved human, is he able to forgive Ivanov of the most heinous acts?

Nobility Dreya Love Book 5 ~ Simon and the team pursue a betrayal from his past and stumble upon a diabolical plot for global genocide.

As they endeavor to stop this catastrophe, clues lead them to a prominent list of participants ... all above the law.

In this thrilling final book in the series, the team comes to understand what it means to be a pack ... and to be Nobilized.

Find your heroes in this reverse harem, shifter, crime thriller series. A strong intelligent woman, three alpha males, an inseparable pack. If you want deep romance slow burning until it catches fire, with enough twists to keep you on your toes, you'll love Dreya Love!

Other novels in English by Dana Lyons:

Heart of the Druae ~ Archaeologist Eric Beck travels back in time to Stonehenge and meets his soul mate. The results are complications of the heart. Available in audio!

A Love Reborn ~ A modern tale of ancient love, magic, and betrayal. Phoenix Donovan has two new men in her life. One is her killer—from a past life. The other, a lover trying to save her life before she gets killed ... again.

The Rosetta Coin ~ Ancient artifacts, an alien pursuer, and a man haunted by choices he's made, all come together in a life and death confrontation. The Rosetta Coin is also available in audio!

The Road to Babylon ~ In the sequel to The Rosetta Coin, the fulfillment of an ancient prophecy sets the stage for mankind's final showdown with evil. Also available in audio!

Timeless ~ Alex McNeill has lost her husband, Royce. The path to finding him takes her to Ireland ... 1612!

Made in the USA
Middletown, DE
23 June 2023